THE LANTERNFLY
WRITTEN BY JENNA ARCARO

CHAPTER ONE

THE COURTROOM

There I sat in the back row of a packed courtroom waiting for my boyfriend's brother, John Horrocks, to get what was coming to him for murdering those girls. My thoughts flashed over the severity of the crimes as the prosecuting attorney described the murders one after another.   I could see the women crisply in my mind's eye as he continued, emphasizing each syllable. He was attempting and succeeding at getting a rise out of the jury. I watched their faces, so ethnically and sexually varied that the jury box could have been part of a diversity training commercial. The attorney's shiny black shoes danced effortlessly along the floor as he spoke, pacing, producing only a brief, smooth polish of his sole on the tile rather than a thud.   The courtroom was so quiet, I could hear his pants swish with each new sway left to right.

One by one, I saw the jury glance between the attorney and John, trying to connect the heinous story to the pensive, remorseful-looking man on the stand. His head hung low, blue eyes focused on his knees, anxiously rubbing his right thumb over his left thumb nail.

"So brutally attacked," the attorney continued, "leaving blunt-force trauma to the right side of her skull that was so severe, it nearly crushed her skull in half." The jury collectively winced.

To be honest, it didn't look like John had it in him to beat five women to death then toss them into various local rivers like they were unwanted pieces of garbage. John had a five-year-old son and a wife sitting in the courtroom next to me. She knew he was innocent. And somewhere deep down, so did I.

Chapter Two

THE LANTERNFLY

To explain how I got to that courtroom and how I got involved with any of these people, let's start from the beginning. The year was 2018. I remember it well because that was the year I met Sam. We met organically—as if by chance—in a well-lit café almost like a planned "meet cute" in cinema. He wore a green cotton tee shirt loosely tucked into his dark jeans. His brown dress shoes struck me as oddly formal, a reinforced toe marked by a horizontal addition of leather beginning just forward of the laces. He had some sort of Southern charm about him, not necessarily in voice nor accent but simply by his attire, his gentlemanly ways throughout the café and the way he instantly jumped in to open the door for anyone who needed assistance.

I watched him from behind that day, my eyes trailing across the distinct line of his freshly-coiffed mane, marked by the few extra hairs on the back of his neck. He must have just left the barber. Despite my attempts, I couldn't help but notice the way his broad shoulders filled out that shirt in delightful ways. He was ahead of me in line and just as the jamboree of Sunday-morning patrons began to make headway, a woman stepped across my field of vision, interrupting my thoughts and annoying me deeply with her presence. Her unruly brown, curly hair mocked me as she blocked my view of him. She stood in between Sam and I, anxiously tapping her foot to wait for her coffee as if her time was somehow more precious than mine. I allowed her to cut in line, staring angrily at the back of that mop of hair, determining that having a conversation with her would be far more detrimental to my mood than waiting those few extra moments for the Queen of England herself to order a cup of joe.

As she retrieved her coffee, she removed the lid and inspected it, crinkling up her nose in disapproval long before actually seeing the contents of the cup. She decided immediately and loudly that there was simply not enough cream and made sure the barista knew of her mistake. I rolled my eyes at her but couldn't help but stare as she made such a spectacle of herself with everything she did. As she spoke more, her pretentious, tinny voice pierced my eardrums in annoyance almost like an obnoxious squeal of a break. I would more likely voluntarily blow out both eardrums on purpose than listen to her for one more minute. As I further evaluated her from the profile view, I watched her mouth. She had a terrible-looking porcelain-fused-to-metal crown on tooth #5. A dental hygienist by trade, I could not help but notice the travesty that was this woman's smile and how easy it would be for my office to fix it.

My mind wandered to Dr. Brown, one of the associate dentists in the practice at the time. He was an artist in his work and had completed some truly remarkable smile makeovers that would make even the most discriminating cosmetic dentists "ooh and aah" over his work.

"Rochelle!" the barista announced, setting down a white mug with an adorable leaf drawn in cream on top of the latte. I stepped forward to retrieve my order, hoping desperately that the loud, ugly #5 lady wouldn't talk to me as I approached her territory. She clicked her fake finger nails on the counter as she waited, shooting me an angry glance as my hand slid to grip my mug next to hers.

I nestled down in my leather chair where I sat every Sunday morning with my book. It felt better to read my novels among the clatter of a bustling café than alone in the house for some reason. Not that the introvert inside of me had any intention of interacting with anyone in the shop, but the busy white noise was somehow comforting. I set down my latte first, followed by my novel, purse and cell phone; yet, when I made the small movement to slide backward in the large chair comfortably, my foot pulled my purse and the strap of it accidentally looped around the mug. I wasn't quick enough to catch it.

The brown liquid spilled over the side of my falling mug, nearly in slow motion as I helplessly tried to save it from the imminent crash onto the floor. My heart leapt into my throat as it happened, knowing immediately that I was about to create quite the display, drawing an uncomfortable amount of attention to myself. And that mug didn't do a subtle hop across the floor, either. It shattered into about twenty shards, loudly pummeling the tile floor in an obscene crack that caused curious heads to whirl my way in unison. I looked up, guilty, cheeks flushed as I strolled toward the napkins.

Sam smirked and immediately made his way over to me. The way my face instantly turned red from embarrassment after the crash made his heart soar. In the same way a person has to grit their teeth sometimes when petting a dog just to control the level of affection for that delicate little creature, Sam felt that way about me.

Of course, I had no idea of this at the time. He had been watching me, too.

"I'm Sam," he announced after the mess was cleaned and held out a hand. I shook it and introduced myself politely.

"Rochelle. Everyone calls me 'Ro.'"

His eyes twinkled in the light glaring loudly through the floor-to-ceiling window on one side of us. They were a piercing shade of green. He squinted.

"What are you reading?" he asked innocently, confidently taking the seat next to mine. His chin motioned to my novel on the table.

"Ah, it's another James Patterson crime novel, as usual." I chuckled nervously. "Do you like to read?" I hoped his answer would be affirmative. It would be just my luck to find a handsome fellow without so much as two neurons to rub together to make a third between those ears.

His brow furrowed as he focused intently toward his shoes for a moment.

"Ah, I remember." His brow eased. "Derailed. It was the last book I read. Finished it about a month or so ago but I travel a lot with work. Sometimes I find it difficult to find the time."

"I've read it," I gleamed. Now, to be fair, I have read most things. Aside from professional sports-player autobiographies which interest me in absolutely no way, I can devour a library fiction section like a lion on an antelope. Actually, his pick was an excellent choice. It was one of my favorites: twisty, dark, impossible to predict.

"So, where are you from, Sam? I can tell you're not from Pennsylvania." He instantly laughed.

"And how, may I ask, can you be so sure?"

"You have tucked a tee shirt into jeans. That's not a Pennsylvania thing." I smirked at him flirtatiously. His smile was to die for. Clean. White. Straight.

"You caught me. I'm originally from Texas but I moved here when I was fifteen.

Hence, I've (hopefully) lost the accent." He paused. "And, for the record, you tuck your shirt into your pants because you don't want to get it caught on the damn saddle when you're dismounting a horse. Not to mention when you're shovelin' the stalls and somebody misses where they're throwin'— you don't want to get that hay and poop down the back of your pants." He started nodding, staring off in the distance as if to remember an incident. He swiveled his head back at me. "Trust me."

I could not stop laughing at the whole shovelin' and throwin' twang. "So," I controlled my giggle, "why would you continue to need to tuck in your shirt if you moved from Texas when you were twelve? There aren't many horses around here." He scoffed.

"'Course there are! My parents have a little farm just down the road. I worked in the stalls with those horses my whole life, back in Pearland and right here in Lansdale. My brother, too." His face dropped a bit and his voice became more hollow, "but he doesn't live nearby anymore."

I missed the cues on that. I noticed the change in tone and the expression, of

course, but I assumed it was some sad familial
story that was a little too personal for an
acquaintance. I didn't ask. We continued our
conversation for three hours, laughing,
covering as many topics as possible without an
awkward pause, not even once.   I was so
intrigued by him and couldn't control my
eyes from scanning the lines of his body,
processing how painfully sexy he was and
how I couldn't believe he was sitting there
talking to me.   Eventually, we ordered two
more lattes, shared a muffin and exchanged
phone numbers, making plans to meet up
again.

He was one of those people you meet
that makes you feel like you've been friends
forever and that there isn't enough time in
the day to get to know them.   The sense of
humor is the same and they effortlessly pick
up on each of your well-timed dry jokes,
snowballing off of them in a sea of meme
references and dad jokes.   Falling asleep is
an inconvenience not only because it is time
spent away from the back-and-forth of
sharing stories, but the dreams are not as
fulfilling as real life when you're together.

As we left the café, I took a deep
breath in the summer air, listening to the

fluctuating wave of buzzing from the cicadas in the trees. I thought about how strange it is that their cacophonous noise becomes so familiar that the ears hardly even acknowledge it anymore; that harmonious rise and dip echoing in the distance somehow blends in and begins to sound like silence. I pointed out a red Spotted lanternfly on the outside of the door.

"I know everyone hates those bugs," I leaned in closer to it, "but I think they're beautiful. The colors. They're so intricate with their red underwings and little polka-dots." I smirked at it as I tipped my head to the side to contemplate its existence a while longer. "I love the way they are so harmless but yet so unbelievably destructive like a wolf in sheep's clothing."

Almost in acknowledgement of its mention, it flew and landed right on the pocket of Sam's tee shirt, just above his right pec. I swatted it for him but it evaded my hand and instead made a direct bee line for my face, hitting loudly on my left cheek as I shrieked and dropped everything I was carrying. I leaned forward to try to remove it from where it had landed on the front of my shirt and it got lodged in my long hair as it tried to get away.

"Oh my god!" I continued to scream as I twisted and twirled, swatting at the air with my eyes closed. I could hear its wings battling my hair for freedom. As Sam came to my rescue, I accidentally swatted him right in the face in a full-blown bitch slap, savagely battering him right across the cheek. My eyes shot open when I felt the skin beneath my palm. For a second, I forgot the lanternfly. Sam was too important.

When my eyes finally focused on his face, it became evident that he was laughing. In fact, the two of us began a little dance of laughter right there outside the café, his breathy chuckle urging me to laugh harder and my feminine wheeze worsening his hysteria similarly.

"Beautiful, huh?" he managed to say between breaths. As we continued our whoops, a distinct palm print began to develop in red on his right cheek, which only ripped the air from my lungs in an even more relentless wave of cackling. Eventually, he tipped his chin back and allowed a loud, unrestrained, resonant guffaw to emit from his throat before we managed to pull ourselves together. As he tipped his head back and his lip naturally pulled far above his teeth, I noticed he had some inflammation around the gums of his upper right canine tooth. They didn't look red or anything but just a little raised and inflamed right at the top gumline like he needed a good cleaning from a great hygienist. I made a mental note that I would bring him into my chair once we started dating.

I immediately reeled myself in from my hygiene assessment and allowed him to walk me to my car. We had already made plans to go to dinner that Thursday evening.

"Well, I will readily admit to you, Ms. Rochelle, that meeting you was the highlight of my time here in Pennsylvania and I've been here for twenty-five years." His eyes crinkled a bit at the sides as he smiled down at me.

"Until Thursday," I noted as I ducked into my small sedan. I hoped Sam wouldn't notice the three long drips of dried saliva down the passenger window of my car, forever immortalizing my Labrador retriever's unique talent of territorially marking everything she touches.

I strolled into the house that afternoon after my first meeting with Sam and I couldn't get him out of my head. I patted Luna, my chocolate Lab, on the head as I hauled my things through the front door. She felt it necessary to jump up to my level in order to greet me properly, putting both paws on my chest, nearly pushing my back against the front door by her weight.

"Luna!" I exclaimed helplessly, using my left knee to push her off of me. "Can I please just get in the door first?" I made a mental note to further explore "diet" dry dog foods in the near future. I walked over to her food canister and measured out a cup of food while she quickly developed her signature strings of drool on both sides of her floppy jowls. Sometimes, they would get so long that the movement of her face watching me add food to her bowl would somehow link the strings together in a disgusting pseudo-beard of ropy saliva.

I sat down at my computer. I plugged Sam Horrocks into a search engine. Works for an engineering firm nearby. Graduated high school in 1998. Went to Ursinus college—also nearby. Nothing alarming. No criminal history that I could find so that was a relief; he passed my initial screening. You would be amazed what dirt you can find on someone if you look hard enough.

Months passed and as the moon waxed and waned, I remained—in love with Sam. The love erupted first in lust, a mutual level of desire never previously achieved with any prior romantic partner. The connection between us was nearly spiritual in its birth, beginning immediately and ever-mounting. Each new day adding to our connection through shared experiences: our events, our inside jokes, our memories. How sweet that spiral of love, though downward, can take us. Far into the depths of the unknown as we continue, hoping and praying that it never ends.

It went from summer to approaching fall in no time. The leaves turned by the day, my morning commute becoming more and more picturesque in the morning sunlight. I reveled in the ability to sit at a stoplight on the way into the office just watching a delicate drip of dew dangle from the tip of a yellow leaf in the morning rays of sun. I fall in love every fall and not necessarily with a person. With Pennsylvania.

CHAPTER THREE

RUSTY

Sam had invited me to meet his parents after our first few months of dating and I had nervously agreed. As I pulled up to Sam's parents' farm, a cloud of dust emanated from my wheels as I loudly progressed down the dirt driveway. The fields surrounding the house were colossal in size, almost emulating a vibe of an old plantation house somewhere in the deep south. I saw Sam's truck from the street so I knew I had the right house. There was a beautiful horse in the field to my left who seemed quite interested in my presence, following the car in an excited trot. I parked facing the field and decided to approach the fence to give the horse a friendly pet on the nose.

Just as the horse breached the level of the fence and my hand rested just between its nostrils, Sam's voice boomed from behind me, making me jump.

"You gotta watch her. Name's Rusty. She can be pretty spicy when you turn around if you don't have any treats for her. She knows we keep the grain in our back pocket so when you turn around, she'll nip you in the ass if you stiff her out of her treat."

I was undeterred. She was so stunning and startlingly massive in size that I couldn't pull myself away from the tender moment of simply petting her along the jaw, down between her eyes and on her soft nose. I stared at her long eyelashes as her eyelids began to close. She allowed them to shut about half-way, nearly napping standing up as she accepted my affectionate strokes.

"Wow," Sam remarked, turning his face to gaze upon my pink skin. I met his eyes for a moment. I had put some sparkled bronzer on my face and he brushed a finger across the apple of my cheek to acknowledge the change. He looked back at Rusty. "She really seems to like you. She usually doesn't approach anyone unless they smell like food." I smiled.

While the house itself was very traditional, the barn looked just about brand new. It had modern, wide-open runs for the horses that I could see from the other side of the fence—ones that allowed them in or out of their stalls as they pleased, letting them retreat for cover if they wanted a break from the sun throughout the day. It reminded me of a friend's house from childhood who had a farm. We spent many hours in that barn of hers, playing with the animals and concocting strange mixtures of grain and water in jars for no reason other than boredom. We would only find those jars years later, grown black and moldy on a shelf.

"Maybe horses are like dogs. They are a good judge of character." I smiled.

"You ready for this family dinner?" he said softly, glancing back at the large white farmhouse with a wrap-around porch. His left hand brushed the small of my back.

"I think so. It's just your mom, dad and us, right? Any topics I should avoid?" I asked honestly.

"Yes, just us. Not that you would but probably not a good idea to bring up my brother." He quickly allowed his hand on my back to pull me harder to change the subject. "Come on, let's go inside."

As we turned away from Rusty, she reluctantly pulled her head back over the fence and walked along with us to the corner of her fence, staring as we walked up the steps to the front porch.

"That's so odd," Sam began, staring back at Rusty as she started to whinny and neigh loudly at us. I waved at her.

"Bye, honey!" I chirped.

"I have been working with this horse for ten years and you meet her for one minute, suddenly it's love at first sight. She didn't even try to bite you!" He shook his head.

"Like I said, just like a dog. They get a vibe from people. She knows I won't hurt her; she must just hate you, I guess," I said jokingly.

"Hey—" he began before we were greeted by his mother coming through the front door. We hadn't even knocked yet.

"I'm so glad you're here!" She immediately enveloped me in a hug. She wore a pair of Wrangler jeans and a blouse, also tucked down into her pants just like Sam. "You'll have to excuse me; I just came back in from the yard and I just have to change." She fought the urge to pinch Sam on the cheek. "Get this girl a drink, will you?" she ordered Sam as she started to walk up the large staircase to our left. The wood creaked in a charming, lived-in farmhouse kind of way as she made her way to the second floor. She motioned to the large liquor cabinet just beyond the foyer when going toward the kitchen. "Anything you want, sweetheart. Make yourself at home."

"Nice to see you too, mom." Sam snickered.

"Oh, for heaven's sake," she started from the second floor, the rest of her rant muffled by our footsteps into the kitchen as Sam ignored her. He loved winding her up.

His dad sat at the head of the sturdy wooden table, sipping what appeared to be scotch or whiskey in a short ball glass with no ice.

"Hey there, kiddo," his dad hilariously addressed Sam, standing up and giving him a hug. He had a salt and pepper mustache that looked so perfectly full it almost looked fake.

"Hey, Pops," Sam returned as they both loudly patted each other on the back during the embrace, a hollow noise echoing through their bodies. Maybe they didn't want to seem soft by hugging so they made it manlier by violently hitting each other during the hug.

"And this must be Rochelle," his dad reached out a hand.

"Pleasure to meet you," I responded with a shake and a smile. He had calluses from years of working on the farm, his grip firm. My fingers nearly disappeared in his as his palm was large enough to wrap almost entirely around my hand. His eyes were piercingly blue.

"Call me Joe," he said sweetly.

Sam made me a quick Manhattan in a shaker as I covered the first few topics with his dad.   His mom, Maureen, was still upstairs dressing.

"So, what do you do?" his dad asked innocently.

"I'm a dental hygienist."

"A what?" Sam's shaker continued.

"A hygienist!" I screeched over the noise of the ice.

"Sorry!" Sam announced from the kitchen.

"Ah, well you're going to have your hands full in this family.   Our teeth are a mess." He started to chuckle. Sam shuffled in the kitchen with his back toward us and cleared his throat. "You alright in there, kid?" his dad yelled to Sam but didn't wait long enough to listen to his response. "I'm missing five teeth. Can you believe that? Five. That's why my smile is all crooked. They didn't have braces back then. Well, they did.   But we weren't rich enough to get them." Sam strolled back in with a glass of red wine in one hand and a cocktail for me in the other. "Nope, not like the kids today." He grabbed Sam by the face and Sam smiled. "See that? Five-thousand-dollar smile. Braces."

"So, dad, what do you need me for next weekend?" Sam quickly interjected.

"Oh, the attorney is coming over," his dad anxiously glanced at me. "I thought you might want to be here."

Sam nodded and said nothing more. His mom strolled in with a conservative floral dress and sandals.

"Oh, good," she said, looking at my drink. "I was afraid you might be one of them girls who don't drink." She chuckled loudly to herself as she poured herself a glass from Sam's wine bottle. "Let's eat," she announced and began to unload her previously prepped dishes from the refrigerator, all in colored bowls with tin foil to keep them sealed. I instantly stood to help in the kitchen while Sam and his dad continued in muffled tones at the table. Maureen and I made small talk in while we prepped a few large serving bowls to take to the table.

"Attorney for what?" I wondered to myself.

As the dinner progressed and started to wind down to dessert wine, I was feeling tipsy.

It was fascinating to listen to the stories about life as a farmer back in Texas from Joe and Maureen.

"Back in those days, you could make a living that way," Joe's tired eyes dropped to his plate, "but it just got too hard.   You can't predict it.   One year, you had great crops: food on the table, money in the wallet. And the next year, too much rain or not enough, then people wanted organics but we lost so many to the bugs that way."   Maureen tapped his hand on the table and they locked eyes.   They both turned back to me simultaneously. "We tried."

They had retreated here from Texas for Joe to take a job for a major farming corporation, the exact kind of business that put his small farm out of business. I observed Joe's face, his leathery brown skin from years of sunburn and deep wrinkles around his eyes. His hair was white by this point but his beard still had flecks of the brown it used to be.   I could almost make out what he might have looked like thirty years ago as a young man tending to the farm.

I couldn't decide if Sam looked more like Joe or Maureen.   He had a shimmer of both in his appearance; his thick mane of hair was definitely from his father but his kind, green eyes were Maureen. When he smiled, the shape of his mouth resembled Joe in every way. I wondered if Sam and I had kids, would they be the same way? Would they have my hair and his eyes, his humor and my quick wit? I couldn't imagine how much I could love something that embodied all the things I love about myself intertwined with the lovely qualities of Sam.

"I had a family," Joe continued. He almost looked like he was going to cry. "I had two boys. They needed new shoes for school. They needed swim lessons or cleats for football. I had to."

"So," Maureen chipped in optimistically, "we settled for our own little farm here. We could still get our fill of the animals and the vegetables from the garden, without all the worry about money." Joe threw his head back and laughed.

"All's we got left of the animals is that old broad, Rusty, and damn it to hell do I hate that horse!" We all erupted in laughter.
As we finished up the delicious made-from-scratch peach cobbler, I helped with the dishes.

"Oh, just set 'em in the sink, honey," Maureen instructed as she wrapped the leftovers to put back in the refrigerator. "I'll get 'em tomorrow." She came over and wrapped a hand around my left shoulder while she pressed up against my right in a squeeze of affection. "I'm so glad we finally got to meet you. Come back any time, you hear?"

Sam and I said our goodbyes, gave our hugs and headed to our cars. There was a loud thump of hooves following us from the other side of the fence all the way to the car. He leaned in to kiss me.

"It was love at first sight for me, too, you know, not just Rusty," he whispered. Our lips pressed, him backing me up into the side of his truck. His hand lifted to grab my face and move it to the left, exposing my neck for him to bite. I felt his tongue move up the delicate skin of my neck, eventually swirling around my ear.

My skin prickled at the sensation. His hands instantly slid underneath the hem of my dress and immediately my panties were dangling between my knees. With one movement of his hand, he had encouraged me to spread my legs more. I glanced back at the house. It felt a little inappropriate being within earshot of his parents' front door. He didn't seem concerned. We were on the opposite side of the truck so at least we were obscured from view. His fingers teased and dipped, heightening me to the point of muffling a moan.

"Let's go back to your place," I suggested between labored breaths. He stopped immediately and smiled.

He instantly kneeled in front of me, using both hands to slowly pull my panties back up into place. He kissed the front triangle of fabric.

"Let's go."

CHAPTER FOUR

LOVE

We stumbled into his house like horny teenagers while their parents ran to the grocery store: urgent, unbridled. Our mouths met over and over again, each new swish of his tongue against mine echoing in a tingle from my lips to my nipples, then down between my legs.

I was nervous. As he laid me down on the couch, I took a quick glance around his house. It was tidy enough for a bachelor. I didn't see any major red flags like that time I walked into a guy's apartment and he had hundreds of assorted Star Wars collectible mugs lining every windowsill with a succulent plant in each. I had faked a mysterious illness and nearly lit my sandals on fire with friction as I ran back to my car to retreat. Never again would I trust online dating after the "succulent incident" as it would come to be called amongst my girlfriends.

Sam's lips were full and soft as he lifted my shirt above my head. His mouth found the crease between my breasts as he reached a hand around and effortlessly unhooked my bra from behind. It fell to the side as he continued downward, looking up periodically to make sure it was okay for him to continue.

I nodded at him from above, running my fingers affectionately through his soft brown hair. He paused to remove his tee shirt, sliding it out from the waistline of his jeans and up over his muscular frame. I shamelessly admired as it fell to the floor next to the coffee table.

He redirected, coming back up to kiss me for a few minutes longer, teasing with his fingers, listening to my breath and when my panting became moaning, he stood. He unbuckled his belt, the button, the zipper, slid his pants to his ankles and stepped out of them. He slid down his boxers and turned away from me, walking into a dark hallway naked, leaving me with only the view of his muscular glutes and thighs as a preview of what was down that hallway.

I followed obediently, listening for his steps down the hall as an indicator of where to go. He flipped on a light in a bedroom with a large, burgundy comforter. A California king, no less. I leaned on the edge of the doorway as he laid on his back, right hand under his head to prop himself up to look at me.

It felt so respectful the way it happened. It was as if he was giving me control, letting me decide if I wanted this (though I had driven all the way to his house for this to happen). The way he laid naked in that bed without any force pulling me to him but my own desire, somehow made him seem demure or even a little submissive.

I stepped out of the rest of my clothing and climbed up, sliding my knees across the comforter in a slow crawl toward him. His eyes were so green and intense as he observed every inch of me naked for the first time. Our lips met again and his hand pulled my leg over top of him into a straddle. It felt so right, the way he lifted his hand up to slide it through my hair as we started to rock. I could feel a throbbing pulsation of tension through the tips of my fingers as we continued.

Each fiber in my body buzzed with this strange electric twinge of excitement. I loved him. He looked up at me through the chaos of the bed rocking and met my gaze. He looked so vulnerable underneath my control, admiring me from below like a lovesick puppy.

"You are so beautiful," he managed to whisper.

Our lips met again just as every current of that electricity solidified into one solid, rippling shock that sent me half-way to Texas and back. I leaned over him, panting into his neck, propping myself up on both hands just above either one of his shoulders.

"Dear God," I announced in a breathy, satisfied, exhausted tone. I rolled over onto the other side of the bed and we laid side-by-side, staring up at the ceiling for a while as we caught our breaths. My eyes grew heavy. He slid his left hand over to hold mine.

"Are you on the pill?" he asked out of the blue which caused a choke of laughter to rise from my throat.

"It's a little late to ask." I turned on my pillow to face him and observed the profile of his face. He smiled as his eyes closed, lying comfortably on his back. "Yes, I am." I used my pointer finger to run it from his forehead, down between his brows, over his nose, and down onto his lips. He seemed to enjoy it.

I ran my finger over his left eyebrow, then his right. His eyes remained closed.

"You're going to put me to sleep," he whispered.

"My mom used to do that to me when I was sick," I began. "I would lay on her lap with my head across her lap on the couch and she would rub my hair, then my eyebrows until I fell asleep."

"That sounds sweet," he replied. "Why don't you come a little closer," he outstretched an arm for me to slip underneath, "and I'll see if I can find a better way to put you to sleep."

I slept like a rock under his arm, almost like a weighted blanket to keep me warm and pinned down to prevent me from tossing and turning. In many years, I cannot remember sleeping that soundly.

I woke in the morning in a blurry fog. I had forgotten about Luna! That dog would absolutely burst before she ever went to the bathroom in my house. I glanced at my watch. I left for dinner the night before around 7pm. It was almost twelve hours for her to hold it.

"I have to go," I tried to whisper but did not wait to see if he woke up. I had to split, fast. I closed the door silently, turning the knob all the way to withdraw the latch as I pulled it shut and let go. I didn't want to wake him. It was Saturday.

I raced home in my sedan, obeying a casual twenty miles over the speed limit on every street it took to get back to my place. I threw it in park even before the car coasted to a full stop and in one fell swoop, I withdrew the key, grabbed my items and started an urgent jog toward the front door. Luna stretched and yawned when I walked in, my heart rate dropping in relief that she seemed unconcerned and had not been crossing her legs for the past twelve hours. Phew. She had this look on her face like she knew I had been out and up to no good.

"Don't judge me," I said to her as I fumbled with the clasp of her leash, trying to hook it on her collar. Her brown tail wailed me over and over on the leg as she paced around in a circle. "For Christ's sake, stay still," I mumbled while giggling at her. I finally had to grab her by the neck fat to keep her from moving so I could actually get her on the leash. I kissed her on the head before I opened the door to the backyard.

I stood there, happily peering over the grass of my yard with Luna making circles in the grass deciding where to urinate. It would be a few minutes of consideration before she would choose a spot. I thought about my childhood dog, Jack, and how much I still missed him.

Jack was a black lab and just as mellow, if not more than Luna. He would sit at the edge of our yard without any sort of fence, just knowing that he was not allowed to cross the line of the sidewalk. God, he was a good dog. His mouth would drop into a pant then close, assuming an intense stare when something caught his interest, finally panting again in a relaxed rest on the front grass.

About two weeks before Jack went missing, we had been out in the garden picking weeds when my mother had overheard someone's idle of the car out by the front yard. The trees blocked our ability to see but my mom strolled over, wondering. Maybe someone was having car trouble and needed help, she thought.

"You want him?" she overheard a man saying, talking to his girlfriend through an open pick-up truck window, standing next to Jack. He was all set to steal our childhood dog right then and there.

"Ah-hem" my mom cleared her throat as she made her presence known to them, the man retreating and skidding his tires in his flee.

Yet, two weeks later, Jack went missing and we were never able to get him back. It was such a helpless feeling to have someone you love ripped from your life and never obtain justice for it. You spend so much of your time back-tracking your own behavior, wondering where you could have stopped it and the guilt of it all is almost paralyzing.

We put up signs, offered rewards, posted on internet pages, took out classified ads, all trying to find Jack but we never did. We don't know if he was sold, used as a bait dog, abused, killed. There is a gnawing and constant ache of pain feeling like someone you love is suffering and you can't do anything about it.

I blinked away tears vividly imagining the prickle of the grass against my bare legs as I sat with Jack in the grass, sliding my fingers under his brown leather collar to scratch. He always loved that for some reason and would lean into me, dropping his eyelids in pleasure like I was scratching that one itch he could never reach.

The only person who ever saw the man or the truck was my mom. To this day, I wished I had walked out from the garden with her, had seen him and memorized his face or his license plate. I could feel my hands turn into angry fists right there in my backyard thinking about it; how badly I wanted justice for Jack, to put that man behind bars, or better: to kill him.

As I stood there staring at my arborvitaes in a boiling sear of tormented anguish, a text lit up my phone paired with a short burst of vibration in the back pocket of my jean shorts.

"Hey, you left awfully quickly this morning. Everything ok?" Sam sounded so concerned. I explained the fiasco with Luna's bladder and how I needed to run but couldn't stay to explain.

"I understand completely. Hope Luna is okay now. Do you want to meet for breakfast?" I smiled.

CHAPTER FIVE

THE FIFTH VICTIM

Weeks later, I found myself already in the first week of October and the first Sunday in a few months where I hadn't spent it with Sam. He had gone out of town for work a few days prior, leaving me with all sorts of found time. I could do the laundry I'd been putting off for two months or actually fill a bucket with Lysol and truly cleanse the floors on my hands and knees instead of the typical mid-week sweep to get the gobs of brown hair. The amount of hair that dropped from that adorable fur-ball of mine in just a few days was nauseating. I considered going back to my café which I hadn't done in a while, but eventually decided to stay in with Luna for a change and snuggle with her on the couch.

I made myself a French press coffee and sat down at the coffee table. I turned on the news. Only one channel had news on Sundays but I liked news in the morning. Maybe because it reminded me of my mom. Every morning in middle school and high school, I would hear her television loudly blaring in her room as she shuffled from the bedroom to the bathroom, putting on makeup, changing twice, standing in front of the TV for thirty seconds to watch, then walking back into the bathroom. It was so loud I could hear it from my bedroom at the other end of the second floor.

My mother had been strict right up until I turned eighteen. While our relationship had been pleasant my entire life, always feeling like I could tell her anything, it really blossomed when her presence stopped being so oppressive. We transitioned quickly and seamlessly into close friends. We called each other several times per week. She would tell me tales of my dad as I heartily laughed. This week, he set up three cameras in the backyard to try to catch a glimpse of the raccoons that had been rummaging through the trash at night. The only thing he successfully caught on camera was a loose dog wandering into his yard and taking a shit right within the shot of the lens. As she told me the story, I could hear him mumbling in the background about it.

"Un-freakin'-believable," he exclaimed loudly.

"Have you been watching the news, honey?" my mom asked with that tone of concern I had come to recognize.

"Yes, I have it on right now. Why?"

"They say there was a fifth girl found in your area. She was in her thirties, just like the other girls."

Just as she said it, the television panned to a shot of a river and dozens of people scouring the water. I turned up the volume and we both sat in silence for a minute. The girl had been tossed into the Schuylkill River, about ten miles from my house. Her body, just like the other four women who had been found in the past few months within Montgomery and Bucks county, had been found pretty quickly after her death.

"They think it's the same guy," my mom announced. "I don't know how they know that. Maybe because she was in the river, too."

Now, let me preface this by saying that the only person who is more of a crime savant than myself (thanks, crime novels) is my mother. A crime show addict, one comment about a gun and she could rattle off twenty-five facts about it, including how effective it would be to kill someone.

"Well, the nice thing about a .22," she had started saying once during a dinner out at a public restaurant, "is that it's not powerful enough to go all the way through a body. So,

it just stays in there until they bleed to death."
She washed down the statement with a swig of
beer and another bite of her sandwich, blinking
casually.

"How the hell do you know that?" I
shot back at her, looking at my dad for
verification as he was the gun connoisseur of
the family. He nodded in agreement. My dad
laughed and motioned to her.

"I.D. channel. Just remember: if I ever
go missing, it was her." He motioned to her
with his head. They locked eyes affectionately
and she smirked through her mouthful of
food.

My parents had been dating since the
seventh grade. They broke up once in high
school and dated other people, quickly
deciding that the other options around town
paled in comparison to one another. A year
went by and they gave it another shot—this
one ending in a marriage, two kids and a dog.
I had only ever heard them truly fight once.

Back in my living room, I grew silent
with the phone still pressed to the right side of
my ear. The wrapped gurney on television was
placed into the back of a van marked
"coroner."

"That is really close to here," I remarked accidentally. I would typically stifle those kinds of statements if I could help it; I didn't want to worry her.

"Yeah. You still have your .22?" she asked. I smirked.

"Yes, I do, mom. Hey listen, I have to run. I need to take Luna out for a walk. Let me give you a call later this week."

"Okay, honey. Have a good week. Love you."

I hung up with her and sat on the edge of my brown leather couch to watch the report all over again five minutes later. How mundane it must be to anchor a news channel, I thought, watching the same person repeat the same words I had just heard a few minutes prior: same tone, same expression, same over-enunciation. I wandered into my bedroom and took down my gun safe. I plugged in my code —Luna's birthday—and retrieved my gun. I typically kept the clip loaded but out of the gun.

"Screw it," I decided. I don't have any kids so it's not like anyone in the house other than me would get ahold of it. I loaded the clip. I pulled it up as if I was aiming it at someone standing in the doorway. I pulled back the hammer to load one in the chamber. Then, I set it in my nightstand. It had been a few months since I went target shooting and I wondered in the event of a true emergency, if my hand shaking would impede my ability to aim.

My mind twirled to the time my dad and I had been shooting cans off of a few stumps at our mountain cabin. To use the term "cabin" is a generous; it was really more like a dilapidated trailer on some cinder blocks, complete with mouse poop in the corners of the bedroom because no one was ever up there to clean the place.

"Ping," my shot would echo off the trees as I took down the third Pepsi can. I would scrunch up the fabric of my sweatshirt on my right arm as a pad for the rifle to kick back into my bicep. I was only about ten at the time.

"Remember," my dad said gently after re-setting the cans on the stumps. He grabbed the rifle from me and handed me the .22 caliber pistol that I still have in the house. "If you ever need to use it on a person, wait until they are close enough. Unless they have a gun, avoid the instinct to shoot right away when they're too far. You'll miss and you'll have one less bullet when you need it. Wait for them to come to you. Fewer than fifteen yards, closer if possible." I nodded and closed my right eye. Ping.

CHAPTER SIX

THE ATTORNEY

The following weekend, I met up with Sam at a local bistro we frequented for lunch. They had outdoor seating and in the crisp, fall weather, it was the perfect day for a sweater and a scarf. I relished the sound of the crisp leaves crunching beneath my boots as we looped around the right side of the building. Sam slipped his hand into mine.

Our favorite waitress recognized us and seated us along the brick wall: a table for two. Menus were brought over and placed in front of us. There were only two other patrons seated well over fifty feet away from us.

"What are we drinking?" she asked.

"I'll have a 90-Minute IPA," he replied without hesitation.

"I think I'll have a cosmopolitan today, Wendy. Thank you." She nodded without writing it down and continued inside to the bar.

Sam looked markedly more austere than his typical nature.

"You alright?" I asked.

"I think I need your help." His brows moved upward as he pinched his lips between his teeth and rubbed them together for a moment. He almost looked like he was about to cry. I hitched my head to the side indicating my interest.

"It's my brother, John. He was captured yesterday."

"Captured?" My mind was swimming.

"Yes. He has been a suspect in a case. There have been women disappearing and showing up days later tossed into a river," he began. My eyes widened.

"He was questioned after the second girl disappeared almost a year ago. He got so spooked that he took off. We didn't know where he was for this whole time. But the girls kept disappearing. They have him in custody now."

"Okay," I interjected slowly. "How can I help?"

"So, apparently there have been bite marks. We got an attorney after John told my dad he had been questioned. My dad has been working with the attorney for months already, building a defense, even though we knew John took off. John's not very intelligent. We had a feeling he would be caught eventually."

Wendy came back with our drinks and took our order. We placed them quickly, coldly with an urgency that was irregular for us. No small talk today, Wendy. She retreated into the building again.

"So," he continued, "the good news is that we have almost nine months of a case built already for the first two women. We have time cards, people able to confirm he was in this place at this time—multiple people, even. Coworkers, I mean. They can confirm his dates, even down to the half-hour interval when shifts changed. He was at work so there is no way he could have done it."

I nodded along, still confused as to my role in all of this.

"There have been bite marks on all of the victims. Unique marks. That is why John was questioned in the first place."

"Ah, I understand now."

"Yes, the attorney suggested we get an expert witness for the bite marks. My parents can't afford to pay someone to do it, so I thought you could testify."

"Well," I pondered, almost flattered at the idea. "I could help you. I will need his dental records. Who is his family dentist? John is going to have to release his records to me unless the attorney has special privileges to obtain his records without his consent. I know teeth well, but not so much about law."

"The attorney already has them."

"Okay. Let's see what I can do."

We left that day and went immediately to the law offices of Young and Sterner. The building was rather meager in stature, indicating that their expertise in cases involving anything higher than small claims court was probably nonexistent. If I was John, I might just kiss my own ass goodbye right now.

We walked in to meet John's defense attorney, Mark Riles. Not one of the names on the front door, either. Sam was right. They really were going to need my help.

Sam let us alone for the meeting and sat outside for an hour in a waiting room chair, aimlessly checking emails and social media to keep himself entertained. He spent a few minutes chatting with the receptionist who offered him a candy from her dish. Butterscotch. She wore horrible blue makeup around her eyes with hair so severely starched with AquaNet, she appeared to have walked out of 1985. Gale force winds in a cat five hurricane couldn't move those bangs.

Mark set out the dental records, the pictures of the bite marks on the victims, including the three newest women—all of whom had the same deviation in the bruises left on the corpse. There was no mark left for the permanent maxillary right canine in all of the photos.

I scoured through his dental records, dating back to about 1993 which made sense considering Sam said the family moved here roughly twenty-five years ago.

All dental records for John indicated that he was congenitally missing that same tooth, the upper right canine—#6. However, he had an implant placed as a replacement tooth roughly twenty years ago. He never had the actual tooth put on the implant, just the screw in the bone. After that, he never went back to that dentist for the last step of the implant—the crown.

"So, what other office did he visit after 1999?" I mumbled in annoyance as I flipped back and forth between the charts. This attorney was a joke. How was I supposed to come up with an airtight legal theory with just six years of dental records and absolutely nothing in this decade?

Mark shrugged. "We asked him and he told us he visited a dentist only three or four times since then, down in Philadelphia. He can't remember the name of the practice nor the dentist but claims the dentist retired anyway. So, it's not like we can just call over there. John claims he had the final tooth—"

"It's called an implant crown," I interjected.

"Yes, the implant crown, placed on his implant at this other dentist in Philly."

"When?"

"He claims it was almost twenty years ago—shortly after he had the implant placed. He went to them to get the implant crown because it was cheaper than his regular dentist."

"Ok, I instructed.

"Why don't we call his insurance company that he had at the time. They should have a record of who they were paying for his visits."

"John works in a factory. They don't have dental insurance. That's why he stopped going to the dentist. Once his parents stopped paying for it, he was on his own to pay out-of-pocket. He says he only went for this implant crown and for two or three emergency visits."

"Okay, fine. Find his credit card records from twenty years ago, then. There has to be some sort of paper trail to prove this."

"John said he paid in cash."

I sighed loudly. If we did not have proof that he had the implant crown placed, then the missing #6 on the bite marks is plausible. As far as his current dental records showed, the implant was in the bone only and there would be no mark of an actual tooth in the event that he left a bite.

"I need to examine him," I demanded. Maybe by the type of implant crown it was, we could get a better idea of how old it was. Was it in the last five years or older than that? It was a stretch but it was worth a try. I would need my boss. Hygienists are great at soft tissue diseases but the unique nuances of restorative dentistry, I'll leave that to someone who works elbow-deep in it every day.

Mark handed me some pictures they had taken of his mouth inside the prison. He did, in fact, have an implant crown on #6. When it was placed was a topic of contention but it was there. One other thing struck me about the pictures.

"Here," I motioned to the picture of his smile, upper and lower lips pulled back to show all of the gumlines. "He is left-handed."

"What?" Mark said, grabbing the picture and turning it toward himself on the desk. "How can you tell that just from a picture of his teeth?"

"Here," I pointed to the upper and lower left canines. "See the redness? It's common for people who use a regular toothbrush—not an electric one—to miss this spot. People who are right-handed typically miss the right canines. Are you right-handed, Mark?" He nodded. "When you brush," I grabbed a pen to mimic a toothbrush for emphasis, "you have to bring the entire toothbrush out of your mouth and turn it to go from brushing the right side to the front teeth then down the left of your mouth, see."

He nodded.

"A lot of times, you miss the spot of the canines because it is an awkward angle with your hand."

Mark had turned away from me and was shuffling through other papers in John's file. He showed me the reports of the women from the forensics team. All had been the victim of blunt-force trauma on the right side of the head.

"Does it say if they were facing their attacker or facing away?"

Mark intensely flipped through a few more reports. "Let's see. Oh, here. Judging by the impact of what appeared to be a baseball bat—a bloodied one was found not far from one of the bodies and was consistent with her wounds—the forensics team theorized that all five of the women were facing away from the assailant in the attacks." He leaned forward to show me the picture of the woman's head trauma.

It was a woman's face, blue and waterlogged from her time floating down the river. There was an enormous contusion on the right side of her skull. My face dropped instantly at the picture; I had never seen a body other than a viewing at a funeral home and even then, it made me feel sick.

"I'm sorry," he apologized when he recognized my response.

"No, I'm fine," I chuckled. "I see unpleasant things every day at work just—" my voice trailed upward as I tried to stifle the tears that surged behind my eyes. That was someone's little girl. I cleared my throat. "It's a different kind of unpleasant I guess."

I sat in silence for a few seconds, just pondering the reality of what I was seeing. It's one thing to hear about the crimes but another thing entirely to actually see them in a photograph. I thought about their poor parents, the families of these women and how it must feel to have your daughter ripped away, knowing that she suffered great pain on her way out. Those women—those families— needed justice for this, just like I needed justice for my childhood dog, Jack.

"Right here," Mark pointed gently at the photo. "The skull is more shattered at the front of her skull than the back, indicating that the bat swung and contacted her closer to her forehead first, the skinnier part of the bat making less of an impact on her bone."

"So, it can't be John."

"Well," Mark replied, trying to sound hopeful. "We'll need confirmation of this theory of yours."

CHAPTER SEVEN

JOHN HORROCKS

John was being remanded in custody about thirty minutes away. The prison was strangely nestled in a beautiful countryside with rolling hills and largely spaced, stately homes situated in the surrounding five or so miles.

He was in a grey jumpsuit when they brought him in to talk to me. I had been allowed to bring a flashlight and Dr. Brown sat behind me in a stiff chair. Mark aimlessly paced behind us.

Our eyes met through the glass. He picked up the phone on his right side and I did the same. He was handsome. He looked like a rugged, muscular version of Sam. Eyes were blue though, not green like Sam and Maureen. I broke the silence first.

"Hello, John." He nodded, shooting a look to the three of us. He couldn't decide what to make of the motley crew before him. I continued, "This is Dr. Brown. We are in the dental field. We are going to try to help you." His spirits brightened as indicated by the corners of his mouth. He smiled widely. Sure enough, there was an implant crown on #6.

"John, are you sure you can't remember the name of the doctor who placed that crown for you? It would be a great help. Even if he retired, if we could find him. They have to keep records. This could be huge in your case." He shook his head side to side.

"I have tried and tried to think of it but I just can't remember. I only went there a couple times and it was years ago." He motioned to Mark as he continued. "I didn't have any insurance."

"I know. We are going to look in your mouth today, John. We might take some pictures. We are going to try to prove when you had that done. You said about twenty years, right?"

"Yeah," he scratched the back of his head with his left hand. "I'd say about then. I was about eighteen or nineteen."

"So, you're about two years older than Sam" I said accidentally, more processing internally than anything else.

"Sam? How do you know my brother?"

"Oh," I stumbled. "Well, we're friends."

"That's funny," John snarled, "Sam doesn't have many of those. Wonder why."

I cocked my head to the side. Sam hadn't indicated any animosity between them.

"Do you get along with your brother?" I asked innocently.

"Let's just say that Sam only cares about Sam. He'll have some friends, sure. Especially at work. He'll make good with anybody he has to so long as he gets what he wants out of 'em. Then he'll drop 'em like a bag of mulch when they stop being any use to him. He's like a chameleon that way. One minute he's Mr. Southern Charm. The next, Mr. Stuffy Suit. Just depends who he needs to impress."

I was taken aback. Come to think of it, Sam hadn't introduced me to any of his friends. He'd met all of mine.

"He's smarter than you," John remarked matter-of-factly.

"Sam?"

"Yes." I was offended. Maybe it was the blonde hair and the typical assumption that I was an idiot. Call me ugly all you want but don't ever accuse me of being stupid.

"I doubt that" I shot back, smirking. I quickly changed the subject and we shuffled into a room to assess his teeth. We were allowed only to bring a mirror and a flashlight to assess his implant.

Dr. Brown spoke first.

"I mean, it's impossible to tell the kind of implant unless we actually take the implant crown off and look at the implant itself," Dr. Brown said, mostly to me. "But judging by the x-rays and the appearance of the crown, I'd say it is most likely a Nobel or a Straumann implant, both of which were available twenty years ago. It's not going to help us much to determine the kind of implant. It's an extremely common type. He could very well have had it done two decades or six months ago. Without the record of service, there is no way to tell."

I nodded. It was a failure but it was worth a try.

A thought popped into my head. It wouldn't necessarily prove anything since he could have had something removable this whole time—a partial denture, or something like a nesbit partial that only replaces one tooth. He could wear it during the day and just take it out at night. But maybe we could ask his coworkers. Did John go twenty years without a tooth? Or, when he showed up to work in the morning fifteen, twenty years ago, did he have #6?

"John, do you have someone who you have worked with for a long time? Someone who sees you every day?"

"Yeah, a couple." Mark handed him a paper and a pen. He furiously wrote on the paper.

Eric Clemens. Theresa Jones. Ray Carole. Mark shot me a look. Left-handed.

CHAPTER EIGHT

THE CASE

After proving my worth to Mark, he kept me on the case to help him along. As I had anticipated, this was Mark's first murder trial and he was extremely unprepared. I kept demanding records he did not have, testimonies of which he had not yet thought.

"So, here's what we know," I began in front of a whiteboard in a conference room of the law office. I separated the board into two sections, left and right.

On the left side, I wrote significant parts of the case. "All five women were killed in the past year. They were all in their late thirties and they all had a unique bite mark. They were all tossed into some sort of body of water—mostly rivers and just one into a lake. They were all within a 60-mile radius. They all had blunt-force-trauma to the right side of their head." On the right side, I wrote whether or not the key elements of the case aligned with John.

"John is roughly the same age as most of the victims, give or take a few years. John is congenitally missing #6. No connection to the lakes. John has resided within the geographic zone of the murders for years. John is left-handed."

"And," Mark added. "John's alibi checks out for the first two murders. His time cards match up and we have three people who can verify he was in the building at the beginning, middle and end of his shift on the two days where the forensics team determined the time frame of death occurred. The last three murders, however, he was off-the-grid and no one can verify his whereabouts."

"Wait. I stared at the whiteboard for a moment. Why was John questioned in the first place? I know he is missing the very tooth that does not show up in the bite marks but there is no way to search for that. His old dental office would not have been able to run a search for charts of people who are congenitally missing that tooth. I mean, maybe there is a way but I wouldn't know how to run a search like that with Dentrix."

"What's Dentrix?"

"It's a dental software" I replied. "Anyway, how else was he connected to the first two murders?"

"Oh," Mark began with a look of guilt on his face. "When they started looking into the first murder—that of Sherry Kriebel—that was Mark's girlfriend at the time."

"I see."

"When they looked back into his records and saw the tooth thing, they thought they had him nailed to the coffin."

I felt a cold chill run up and down my spine. Something was wrong. Something about this case wasn't right but I couldn't put my finger on it.

"Did he know any of the other women?"

Mark shook his head. "No."

"Were any of the women connected in some way?"

"Two of them attended the same high school."

"What high school was that?"

"North Penn."

"The others?"

"Souderton, Quakertown and Christopher Dock."

"Year of graduation?" He glanced down at his papers.

"Varied. All between 1995-2000."

"Where did John go to high school and what year did he graduate?" I turned away, looking back at my board.

"North Penn. 1996."

I started drawing a flower with my marker on the board as I dipped into my thoughts.

"Rochelle," Mark called to wake me from my thought process as Sam used his pointer finger to rap on the glass of the conference room. He was my ride.

"Rochelle!" Mark called louder.

I spun around wildly, capping the pen and placing it next to the eraser on a ledge about waist-high.

"We need a phone book. Philadelphia. From 1999."

CHAPTER NINE

THE SILVER BULLET

After a significant amount of searching, we were unable to locate a physical phone book from 1999 for the Philadelphia area. The best we could manage was to order one from an online service but delivery would take several weeks. I decided to make a call to one of my professors from college who happened to be from the Philadelphia area.

"Do you remember any dental practices in the area at the time? By name, perhaps."

"Well, my family dental office was Dr. Smith but I doubt that's going to help you narrow it down. There were a few other offices in town but I can't remember them off the top of my head." I gave her some information about why we were pursuing the information.

"Wow," she remarked followed by a long pause. "Rochelle, I am going to visit my mother tomorrow who lives in the city. I'll ask her. She doesn't remember that well since she is elderly but you never know with her. Ask her how many blue pills she took that morning and she can't recall but ask her what color suit Jackie Kennedy wore to some event and she'll rattle it off in two seconds flat. I'll call you after I see her. I'll write them down if she remembers."

"Thank you so much! I appreciate that. We chatted for a few more minutes about my life after college. My boyfriend. Her husband had passed since I graduated so she was still getting used to living alone.

"Until tomorrow," I reminded.

"Yes. Talk soon." We hung up.

I left the house and went to Mark's office again. We had planned to meet around one in the afternoon and I arrived on the dot. His shiny black Mercedes slid into the spot next to mine and he waved at me through the window. We walked in together from the parking lot, him casually strolling in with his coffee tumbler. He wore a silver wedding band on his left hand. It was Saturday.

"Doesn't your wife get mad that you're working all the time, even on weekends?" He threw his head back and laughed as he slid his silver key in the slot on the door of the office.

"No. She's a saint. I mean that. I've never met anyone like her in my whole life. I'm blessed that she even bothered to look my way in high school."

"Aw," I swooned. "You were high school sweethearts?"

"Yes, you could say that. She had a bit of a wild streak in high school and she was hard to pin down but I was persistent." He adjusted his glasses as he sat down in his office, facing me across the desk. "She's a wonderful mother. I couldn't do it without her."

Just then, my phone rang. I didn't recognize the number.

"Hello?" I answered hollowly.

"Hey, Rochelle. It's Professor Tate again." She sounded excited, even giddy.

"I arrived at my mom's house about a half hour ago and asked her about the dentists in the area." I held my breath. "You're not going to believe this. She has one. She rummaged through some old cabinets and I followed her to see what she was doing. She has stacks of them. She kept every phone book from the last twenty years. I have 1999."

We followed up on every lead from every dentist in Philadelphia around the year of 1999. Some of them still lived in the same houses listed in the phone book at the time. Some still had a house phone with the same number.

It was nearly five o'clock that evening when we finally made the call to Dr. Ross. We were nearing the end of our list and finding it very discouraging to that point.

"Do you want to order a pizza?" Mark asked me as the phone continued to ring in my ear. I nodded.

Dr. Ross answered.

"Hello?"

I hadn't anticipated him picking up and I was still a little distracted from the pizza question. I stumbled.

"Um, hi. Yes, is this Dr. Ross?"

"Speaking?"

"Hello, Dr. Ross.   My name is Rochelle.   I am calling because I found your number in our list of dentists that have retired in the Philadelphia area.   I, er, we are calling to obtain dental records for someone who may have been a former patient if yours.   It is pertinent to a legal case."

To our surprise, Dr. Ross sounded much more energetic than the last fifty or so phone calls.   He seemed excited to talk about the good old days of dentistry.

"Do you recognize the name John Horrocks?" I asked.

"Hm, it has been a while, you understand," he responded contemplatively. "But that name rings a bell for some reason." He paused for a second.   "You're not the first person to call me about this person."

"We're not?" I reacted instantly.

"No, about a year ago, maybe less. Some guy called asking about his records and I did find them in my stack."

My heart dipped to my knees. What a manipulative little vole that John Horrocks. Cute routine. "I can't remember, blah, blah." Give me a break. He did it. That piece of crap did it and he played us all.

"Did you give him the records?"

"No. I told him even though I only have to keep them for five years, I kept all of them. Paper charts, of course. None of this digital nonsense. But the law still applies. He needed to have proof of identity or a legal release of records. That stopped him pretty quickly. He was all set to come down here and get them but once I told him I wouldn't give him anything without a valid photo ID, he came up with some excuse why he couldn't make it. Sounded pretty odd to me."

So, it wasn't John who called. Maybe Sam's dad? Sam? Why would they have wanted his records? Why wouldn't they have given us the name of this other dentist?

"We need those records and we have proof of ID."

We set up a meeting with Dr. Ross for the following day and he didn't disappoint. He answered the door to his rather elegant center-city home wearing a casual pair of khakis and a white polo shirt. His beard was completely white but tamed. Rolex watch.

As we entered the heavy wooden door, he led us into the kitchen and we exchanged the ID and a release-of-records form signed and dated by John. We explained to Dr. Ross the circumstances of needing the files. He nodded.

"They say the dental records are kept for the purpose of identifying a body in the case of an accident which is why I always kept these records here in the basement. I just never thought it would help keep an innocent man out of jail." And with that, he produced the thin, 9X11 manila folder with a metal clasp at the top to keep the papers and x-rays nailed down to the file. It was all there—radiographs (x-rays), clinical notes, ledgers—everything we needed, all in tip-top shape. I held up the panoramic x-ray to the light and smiled from ear-to-ear.

We had the record of service, the ledger indicating his cash payment and a perfectly intact radiograph proving that John

Horrocks had a permanent implant crown placed on August 7th, 2000.

I called Sam to tell him the good news.

"It's odd, though," I started to probe. "Dr. Ross said someone else called about his files several months ago but couldn't prove identity." I was waiting for a hitch in his tone, something to tell me that maybe Sam knew something about this case that I didn't.

"Probably the prosecuting attorney for Sherry," he answered without skipping a beat. "He's the district attorney so I'm sure he has loads of connections. I don't know how he would have found the dentist but both attorneys by law have to have access to the same information. Both attorneys knew there was a bite and knew he was dating Sherry at the time." True. It still didn't explain why the DA didn't pursue it further; they can subpoena any records they want, consented or not—right?

"You may have just saved the day, Ms. Lanternfly," he replied with emphasis on that southern accent he did on occasion. I chuckled. He had never let me forget that first date of ours, being molested by that bug just seconds after exclaiming about its beauty.

"I'm going over to the farm tonight for dinner. Mom's making steak. You hungry?"

"Sure am," I replied. We settled on a time and as I pulled up to the house, Rusty galloped toward my car.

"Hey there, sweetie," I acknowledged as she stuck her face over the fence to greet me. I nuzzled my cheek against her nose. She leaned into it.

Sam's footsteps on the dirt behind me alerted me to his presence so the sound of his voice hadn't startled me this time. He enveloped me from behind, kissing my neck and inhaling my perfume.

"God, you smell good," he mumbled as he turned me around to kiss him. He smiled down at me. "I'm so glad you're here."

We ate dinner on the back porch, laughing and drinking wine with his parents. His mom had plucked a few flowers from the back thicket of foliage and placed it in a vase on the top of the table for decoration. They were weeds but she obviously didn't know or didn't care. They were such sweet people. If I needed a shirt, his dad would have taken his off in a heartbeat "just 'cause I needed it," as he might say.

I went over the victory with the dental records and his parents sighed in relief. The lower lid of Maureen's eyes filled with tears as she grabbed my hand under the table and affectionately squeezed. One or two drips spilled over the brim of her eyelid onto her cheek.

"I knew he couldn't have done this," she said, glancing to her husband across the table. "John doesn't have a mean bone in his whole body." She laughed as she looked out over the stable and wiped her cheek with her left hand. "Even with the horses—all the animals, really. He just had a way with them. The one time our stallion got real sick," she turned to me, "and he stayed out there with the damn thing for three days." She laughed back tears. "Heavens to Betsy did he stink when he finally came back inside." Everyone at the table started to giggle.

She wheezed in laughter as she attempted to get out the rest of the story.

"Poor kid slept in poop for three days and I was the mama who let him!" Her kind eyes rested on me. "I just couldn't tear him away. He cried and said he didn't want the stallion to feel alone when he was sick; said he'd stay out there all summer if that's how long it took for Spirit to feel better."

     "He did love that horse," dad chimed in.   He glanced over to Rusty in the field behind the porch. "And then there's this one who'll bite ya in the ass when you clean out her stall." Rusty let out another loud whinny from the field, this time jumping on her back legs and kicking her front feet in the air. When she came back down, she shuffled her feet around a bit, never losing her aggressive stare at the table from about a hundred yards away.

CHAPTER TEN

The Trial

Weeks passed and I had grown closer to Sam with the trial approaching. I had cautioned both Sam and Mark that using me as an expert witness in this case would be poor idea. I did not have a doctorate. I have an associate's degree in applied science and the first thing a prosecuting attorney is going to try to do is discredit my testimony. They need someone with a doctorate—Dr. Brown would do it.

Sam insisted I testify.

"You have a personal connection to this case, now. You know the ins and outs of the assaults, the timeline. It is too close to trial to brief a new person on everything to be prepared in time."

"I agree with him, actually," Mark interrupted. Though Mark and Sam had their fair share of disagreements throughout the process, on this they finally agreed. "It's not going to matter who presents the information that much. The silver bullet is the dental records. We have proof—indisputable proof—that John Horrock's mouth could never create that mark." I nodded. "We have to prepare you for cross examination, though." My stomach sank.

"I have to do that?"

"Of course you have to be cross examined! I thought you said you read a lot of crime novels." My cheeks flushed pink.

"Well I do but part of me hoped that was just in the books. I'm nervous. What if I screw up? Will John go to prison just because I mess up?" I looked frantically at Sam.

He grabbed both of my hands and leaned his face in closer to me, looking me deep in the eyes.

"John is innocent, Ro. I know that and so do you. Nothing you say will change the truth. It will come out. It always does."

It was cold that Monday morning—the first day of the trial. I pulled up to the courthouse with a stomachache the size of Canada. I wasn't even testifying for another three days at least but just being in that courtroom made my hands sweat. I took a seat next to John's wife, Arla and his little boy, Thomas.

"Like the train!" he announced when I asked his name. That was the first time I had gotten the opportunity to meet them. They sat to my left with Sam to my right.

"Relax," he whispered into my right ear, clutching his palm on my right thigh. I smiled. Why was I so tense?

The day passed at a glacial pace. I didn't want to hear the details anymore nor see the pictures. I didn't want to play it over and over in my head like I had been doing for the past few months.

By Thursday, I was exhausted. My dreams had been tormented for days and I woke up unable to stomach a bowl of cereal. Today was the day of my testimony.

I was finally called to the stand, not one hour after the start of the court proceedings.

"I shall call Ms. Rochelle Parks to the stand." Sam gave me one more pat on the thigh.

The blood went everywhere but my face as I stood. It felt like the stand was about three miles from my seat. My shoes echoed in a loud clap with each step, a squeal of the wooden door as it pivoted open for me to take my seat. A cough among the silence.

I sat and faced the room. My eyes fixated on Sam then on Mark. I needed a familiar face.

"Ms. Parks," Mark began, standing and approaching me.

"Can you please list for the jury your credentials as an 'expert witness' in the field of dentistry?"

"Yes. I am a registered dental hygienist with ten years of clinical experience."

"Would you say that qualifies you as an expert in the field of dentistry?"

"I would say it qualifies me as an expert in the field of dental hygiene, if that answers your question." Mark nodded. Just like we practiced.

"I am going to show you a series of exhibits and I'd like for you to familiarize yourself with them so we can discuss them. Please observe exhibit 78: this is a photo of a bite mark left on one of the victims, Sherry Kriebel. Please also observe exhibit 79: an x-ray dated August 7th, 2000 of John Horrocks." I nodded as he continued handing me the photos. They were also displayed on an interactive whiteboard for the jury to view simultaneously. "And finally, exhibit 80. The photo of John's mouth with the lips pulled back."

Mark walked back to his podium to glance over his notes.

"Ms. Parks, do you notice anything interesting about these three photos in relation to this case?"

"Well, yes. It would be impossible for John Horrocks to leave a bite mark that was missing the right permanent maxillary incisor #6. The x-ray indicates he had a permanent replacement, a dental implant and crown, on August 7th of 2000." I paused.

"So, you're saying it would be impossible for the mouth of John Horrocks to create that kind of mark on a human being's skin?"

"Yes. Not to mention the photo of his gums indicates he is most likely left-handed. The assailant in this case is right-handed."

Mark laughed heartily in a sad and fake display, turning to the jury then back to me. So rehearsed.

"How can you tell from a person's mouth that they are left-handed, might I ask?"

I explained it the same way I had to Mark, utilizing my pen to show the way a toothbrush is oriented during brushing habits.

Mark had already prepared written corroboration from three coworkers that John was in fact, left-handed.

"No further questions." Mark smiled affectionately at me. "Thank you, Ms. Parks." I smiled nervously.

The prosecuting attorney stood, looking down at his papers for a moment before stepping toward me. He sized me up as he walked, tilting his head to the side. He seemed quite confident even though I had just taken every ounce of wind from his sails. I smiled.

"Ms. Parks," he began loudly, shuffling his feet a bit as he spoke. My eyes settled on the two-inch cuffs at the bottom of his dress slacks. They were so wide they almost looked comical on his short stature. "Do you have a doctorate in the field of dentistry?

"No." He nodded and glanced at the jury, waiting an annoying amount of time for them to process that information.

"Could you please indicate to the jury the extent of your education in dentistry?"

"I have an associate's degree in applied science from an accredited college in dental hygiene." Mark nodded to me. We anticipated that question. I was doing well so far.

"Ms. Parks, from your clinical experience, could you explain how common it is for a person to be congenitally missing (or missing from birth)" he simplified for the jury, "tooth #6?"

"It is uncommon. That tooth can be missing for a number of reasons, though, not involving missing it from birth."

"Like what?"

"Well, it could be decayed to the point of requiring an extraction though we can usually save a canine. They have long roots. We can usually save it with a root canal instead of extracting it unless cost is an issue." The attorney paused.

"Any other reason?"

"Sure. Impaction. It is a tooth that is commonly 'impacted' or stuck in the bone. It could be lodged somewhere in the bone where it cannot erupt at all."

"Okay. So, in your expert opinion, how likely is it that there is some stranger out there who committed this crime who is also missing, for any reason, tooth #6?"

I glanced toward the door. Three armed officers walked in and planted themselves by the door. No one seemed to notice. I maintained my composure.

"How likely is it for a complete stranger, in the same geographic area, who is also capable of murder, who is also missing #6, to have committed this crime?"

"Yes," he replied gently.

"Unlikely," I replied, improvising. We hadn't practiced this series of questions.

"Could you quantify that for the jury?"

"Quantify? As in give you a percent chance of that happening?"

"Yes, that's what quantify means," he responded condescendingly. I squinted my eyes and angrily stared at him for a solid ten seconds to let him know I wasn't appreciative of his tone. If I could have reached out and slapped that smirk right off of his face, I would have. Attorneys. We didn't know you were a smug jerk until you opened your mouth and eliminated all doubt.

"Extremely low. I don't know. Single digits," I replied.

He turned his back to me and started walking to his podium once again. I could feel my heart beat in my throat. I looked at Sam.

"Unless," I announced, looking down at my lap to summon up the strength to continue talking. He spun so quickly on his dress shoes, he looked like he was dancing at a wedding.

"Unless?"

"It is extremely unlikely for a stranger to be missing that tooth. It would be more likely—a higher percentage—if they were related."

Sam's face turned red. I had turned the tables on him. He was trapped and realized how badly he had underestimated me. I am a dental hygienist, for Christ's sake. That day with the lanternfly, his lip had gone higher than his normal lip line and he had given himself away. Inflamed tissue is red, not pink. That's because it wasn't tissue. It was the edge of a nesbit partial denture, where the lab mimics the color of the gums above the fake tooth to make it blend more in the person's smile. It was made of acrylic and it was removable. With his natural smile line being relatively low on his upper gums, one might never notice.

While finding his dental records had proven to be quite the task without his consent, I was sure of it. His #6 was a nesbit. He killed them; every single one. He had taken the partial out to commit the murders, hoping we would never be able to prove the date John had his implant crown placed. He even tried to access John's files to destroy them. He tried to frame his own brother. And I had known about it for months. I just didn't have the protection I needed outside of this courtroom. I hadn't even told Mark.

Mark adjusted himself nervously in his seat. John leaned forward then glanced back at his wife and smiled. He exchanged a look with Sam. Sam looked back at his parents, seated three seats behind him. You could cut the air with a knife.

"What are you suggesting?" the attorney provoked.

"It is possible—even likely—that John's brother, Sam, is the murderer in this case."

Sam tried to think on his feet. He knew I didn't have access to his dental records because when he attempted to get John's, they required ID and consent. He didn't think I knew for sure. Losing his temper would not be in his best interest. But he would get me back for this.

He had planned for the prosecuting attorney to slaughter me on cross examination, discrediting everything I had, including some dingy x-ray from some washed-up dentist's basement. He had planned this from the beginning, the first day. The café. He had followed me. He played me like a fiddle but in the end, I was smarter than he anticipated. Even if I had figured it out, he thought I would be so blinded by my feelings for him that I would never turn him in. Wrong.

The court room erupted into chatter.

"Order," the mallet pounded on the block as the judge demanded silence.

The prosecuting attorney had a short discussion with a few of the present families then with the defense attorney, me and the judge. He was also the district attorney so he was allowed to call the shots.

"In light of the most recent information in this case," he shot a thankful look to me, "we have decided to drop all charges against John Horrocks."

John immediately broke down into a loud sob as his wife hurdled three pews like a collegiate athlete to embrace him. His son, grey elephant stuffed animal in hand, followed. The judge again had to calm the court room.

"And in with the preponderance of evidence presented, we move to charge Sam Horrocks in the deaths of Sherry Kriebel, Marissa Bergey, Katie Landis, Lauren Turner and Dana Rutherford."

The armed officers in blue moved forward on both ends of Sam's bench to take him into custody. There was some confusion among the officers, the bailiff and the DA over who was taking Sam but John was overwhelmingly thankful, his wife hugging me while spilling tears all over my left shoulder.

Joe and Maureen remained in the back seat of the courtroom until most of the people cleared. They seemed dumbfounded, trying to process the specifics of the case and the mental image of their other son leaving the room in handcuffs. I had an armed escort to my car. I glanced at Joe and Maureen as I left but they did not hold eye contact.

CHAPTER ELEVEN

THE CHICAGO INCIDENT

The week after I had dinner at Sam's parents' house—the time we celebrated the big "win" with finding John's dental records—Sam went out of town again. I had been at his place, sitting on the couch and sipping a cup of tea when he got into the shower.

"Hey, hon," I announced as I went into the bathroom. "The towels just came out of the dryer; I'll just set them here for now." I had planned it all. I dipped into the bathroom for just one second and set a stack of towels on the countertop while my left hand took his phone. If he peeked his head out, it would look like the phone was still there, just underneath the towels. I had watched intently for the past few weeks to memorize the code of his iPhone so I could hack into it when needed.

220198 and I was in. I clicked on his email and sure enough I had his flight confirmation. Chicago, Illinois. Departure out of Philadelphia International Airport at 8pm. Return flight a week and a half later.

I marked the email as "unread" to remain undetected. I slipped back into the bathroom as quietly as possible and just as I slipped the phone under the towels with one hand, I started undressing.

He peeked his head out of the curtain and saw me standing there, stripped down to my panties.

"Well, well," Sam said, eyes scanning my body up and down. "There's plenty of room in here, you know."

I stepped into the shower with him and surprisingly got off almost immediately. There was something hot about all the sneaking around, the high adrenaline situation, having sex with someone who could kill me at any moment. The way his hands would playfully loop around my neck as we made love, knowing that in one second, he could squeeze the life right out of me, was strangely erotic.

I was high on the idea that I was one step ahead of him and I was going to be the one to take him down. I was going to be the one to give those families the sensation of justice I longed for with Jack. It was as if, for the first time, my life purpose was completely clear to me and what I needed to do was so much bigger than myself. It never realistically dawned on me that I was risking my own life in order to do this for in my mind, the reward would be so much greater than the risk. It felt

like every crime show I ever watched or novel
I ever delved into was all preparing me for this
like in some way, my path was always fated to
cross with Sam's.

We got out of the shower and I sat on
the bed in a towel while he finished packing
his suitcase. I watched his movements, his six-
pack abs as he walked around the bedroom
with a towel wrapped around his waist. He had
this delicious tuft of chest hair right between
his pecs that I loved to nuzzle with my cheek
and lips while we made love.

He slipped a shirt over his head and sat
on the edge of the bed to put on his shoes.

"I hate to leave you, Ms. Lanternfly.
He leaned back on the bed, lying on his back
while I planted a long kiss on his lips.

"I'll see you on Wednesday night," I
replied, optimistically.

As we left his house and he made a left
toward the airport, I made a right for home. I
beeped twice.

CHAPTER TWELVE

THE SPY

I boarded a red-eye flight for Chicago, Illinois that same night. I knew exactly why he was going to Chicago and if I was going to survive, I needed hard proof.

I rented a hotel across from his for two nights. I sat with binoculars that Saturday morning and watched every person coming in and out of his skyscraper hotel.

The number of Asian people in that section of town was remarkably high for some reason; it worked in my favor and made it markedly easier to find a pale white guy from Pennsylvania.

At 10:01, I spotted him. Blue baseball cap. Jeans. I already had my shoes on my feet. Here we go.

The beautiful part about following someone in Chicago is it is so populated that you can walk four steps behind someone and there are so many people that remaining inconspicuous is a breeze. I took more precautions than that. I dipped into the entrance of a store here or there just in case he glanced back on occasion. Then I would continue following him from afar, sometimes having to stand on the edge of a sidewalk or a fountain to see over the crowd, looking for the blue cap.

He hung a left down a smaller street and disappeared into a building with a red awning. I went three streets down, made a left and came up on the other side of the building, waiting in the alley for three hours. I knew when he came out, he would make a right out of the building and head back to the hotel.

At that point, I would go in.

Sure enough, he emerged. I followed him far enough toward the hotel that I knew he would not be returning to the building with the red awning, then I went back.

"Hello, yes," I greeted the receptionist. "My name is Rochelle. I am a walk-in and I don't have an appointment but I hope you can accommodate me. I seem to have a toothache."

"Oh, sure. Let me see if we have time." She disappeared into the back as I smiled at a few of the other dental office staff walking by. I glanced at their computer software system. Dentrix. Excellent.

I filled out some forms and was taken back into a room shortly. An image was taken of my perfectly healthy tooth, explaining my imaginary symptoms in the hopes that the assistant would step out of the room to get the doctor. I only needed a minute.

"Let me go get the doctor," she announced as she gathered my paperwork and continued down the hallway. I grabbed the mouse of the computer.

Search by last name. Horrocks. In a time-frame of about thirty seconds, I was able to confirm that Sam Horrocks had been seen for a bridge prep, a permanent solution to his missing #6 to cover his tracks now that he knew John would not be charged with the crime. A bridge was a fake tooth that was cemented to the tooth in front and behind of the missing one, thereby replacing it. His intention by coming to Chicago was to make it as difficult to track as possible, running into the same "which came first, the murder or the tooth" problem that we had with John's dentist in Philadelphia. Sam had even lied to me about where he was going. Said he was off to New York City for this week-and-a-half-long trip of his. Just enough time for the lab to make a permanent bridge and cement it.

I took pictures as I went. The ledger indicating payment—cash, no less. The record of service. The clinical notes.

I clicked out of chart and brought my chart back up on the screen to remain undetected. I even brought up my x-ray she had just taken and left it up on the screen the way she had for the doctor.

On the way out of the office, I scheduled my needed "root canal" with my imaginary symptoms I had described. "Yes, I'll be back next week for that," I assured the treatment coordinator.

Without even returning to the hotel, I headed for the airport. Now that I knew the name of the office, the prosecuting attorney could surely subpoena his records if it made the difference between winning and losing the case against Sam. The pictures on my phone would only be enough to convince him the subpoena was worth it.

I knew the time during the trial when I flipped the tables on him would be the time he was charged—litigation would begin shortly after that point, giving us little time to prepare the case. Not like John, where there was almost a year of preparation time before trial. Sam's trial would only be weeks from his arrest date. I needed to solidify the conviction to keep Sam behind bars and keep my head above the river.

CHAPTER THIRTEEN

THE MOTIVE

The day I had gone over after finding John's dental records, his mom and I had cleared the table after dinner. In the kitchen, she hugged me and thanked me for all that I had done for her family.

"You are like an angel sent from heaven," she continued, rubbing by back as I let the water run over a few dishes in the sink. "'Cause you know, if John didn't do this to Sherry, the person who did is still out there. It's a damn shame, too. Sherry was a nice person, sweet and kind of like you, honey. I even think Sam had a crush on her in high school."

My ears had perked at the comment.

"Did they ever date, Sam and Sherry?" I asked, trying to seem disinterested by dropping things loudly in the sink as I washed them. The white plastic strainer in my hands created a dull thump against the metal basin of the sink.

"No, of course not. Sam didn't have much luck with the ladies, bless his heart." She rubbed her hand over her chest. "He was kind of an awkward kid. Spent a lot of time by himself out in that barn."

"Did he ever date anyone?"

"Yes, one girl in high school. Messed him up real bad. Cheated on him, if I can remember correctly. What was her name? Marissa something. Went to Christopher Dock high school—not where the boys went. It's like a religious school I think. I remember him saying that. They had to keep their relationship a secret because her family was really religious. They didn't date for very long and it was a really long time ago. Anyway, she must not have been that religious because she met another guy and broke his poor little heart."

My eyes fixated on a hardened piece of spaghetti sauce stuck to the side of the casserole dish in front of me. I let the water run over it, hoping to soften it. I had to keep my cool. Marissa Bergey was the fourth victim. After making a positive identification after autopsy, her family had requested her name not been released to the public. Still, John had to have heard that name considering he was being charged with her murder. Didn't he remember her? Or was he just as afraid of Sam as I was?

After we left that night and Sam pressed me up against the car again, there was a nervousness about touching him I hadn't felt before. He scared me and it translated into some sort of sexual electricity; knowing he had the ability—maybe even the plan—to kill me but didn't. Just knowing I was his weak spot, made the sex so much better. From that point forward, as the tensions mounted and as my plan solidified, the sex had heated from an ember to an inferno. Maybe I was just as sick as Sam.

CHAPTER FOURTEEN

THE SURPRISE

I drove home after my armed escort took me to my car the day Sam was arrested. On my way from the courthouse, I needed to drive within a few streets of Sam's parents' farm. I considered stopping by to apologize or something, to talk to John. To somehow free myself of the guilt I felt for putting their family through freeing one son and incarcerating the other.

My mind focused on the two yellow lines between the thick slabs of macadam. What would I say? I pictured Maureen's sweet face and the way her expression always softened when she looked my way. Would she hate me?

My phone started ringing in my purse, on the floor of the passenger seat. I leaned forward to lift it to the passenger seat, glancing back at the road. I kept my eyes on the street as my hand pinched over several items, evaluating their shape. Lipstick tube. Travel deodorant. Phone. Just as I glanced at the number, I felt a thud on the car as my tail end spun out. I had been just about T-boned by a truck. My neck ached. I patted my left ear that seared with pain. Blood.

My door was stuck. I pulled on the lever and pushed harder, with both hands this time. Still wouldn't budge. As my eyes cleared and I glanced through my rear-view mirror, I saw the truck.

It was Sam's. My eyes whirled to the side mirror on the left side of the car and there he was, approaching with what looked like a crow bar in his hand. We locked eyes in the mirror and I immediately leapt over the center console and out the passenger-side door, sprinting in no real direction.

Sam was strong but I was faster.

"Where am I?" I tried to reason in my mind, figuring out where I should go. I was too far from home, too far from any business that would have a gun under the desk like a 7/11 or a Cumberland Farms. The closest thing was the farm. Three quarters of a mile away, maybe less.

I sprinted, feeling my throat growing hot with each labored breath in the cool air. My legs felt numb as I strode, left to right, through thickets of grass that hadn't been mowed in at least a month. There were no other houses. Not a single one. I never noticed how remote the farm was until now.

Just then, I heard a growl behind me. Not a subtle one. A diesel growl. Sam was following me by truck. Through the field I bounded, taking a left into the woods where he couldn't follow. He would either have to park and follow me on foot or turn around and hope he arrived at the house before I did.

A half a mile, I processed in my mind as I ran. The dirt was soft under my feet this deep in the woods, so perpetually covered by the canopy of leaves overhead that most of it was damp, green moss. I can run about a 7-minute mile so a half a mile will be three-and-a-half minutes. Could Sam get to the house in the car in less than three-and-a-half minutes?

Probably not. Unless he drove through fields, the streets to get back to the farm were indirect. It would take him at least five—two to get back to the road and another three to get back to the farm. I could do it. I was sure of it.

How did he get out of the cuffs? I saw them take him out of the courtroom in handcuffs. There were three guards with him, though one of them left his side at some point because that was the one who walked me to my car. So, two guards. How could he escape two guards and a pair of handcuffs?

THE LANTERNFLY

"He's smarter than you." John had told me that the first time we met. Those officers. They came in just when my testimony turned on Sam, but no one knew that was going to happen but me. And, evidently, Sam.

He must have known I was going to flip on him that day and instead of ducking out of the courtroom before my testimony, he decided to make it a stage and all of us merely players just like Shakespeare would've wanted. Those officers were in costume, probably flashing fake police badges to get their way through the metal detectors on the way into the building. Paid a decent chunk of money each, all they had to do was impersonate a law enforcement officer for an hour then disappear forever. It was the world's easiest five, maybe even ten thousand dollars cash. Sam had alluded to the fact that he had a decent nest-egg for a rainy day. What better purpose to use it than to keep yourself out of prison?

It dawned on me as I saw the porch of the farm that I was in real danger of becoming victim #6. The very number of the tooth that would incriminate this bastard was going to be my title as my turn on the news came. "Victim #6 has been identified," the annoying anchor would announce in her obnoxiously dramatic tone, vocally emphasizing each syllable while the shot changed to my body being rammed into a black bag and thrown on a gurney.

I ran up the back steps and pounded on the door. Nothing. I glanced out front to the driveway and realized that Joe's car was not in the driveway. They must have stopped to get something to eat or maybe went to John's house to visit with his wife and son. After all, John had been gone for some time. They needed to catch up.

The gravel popped in the driveway as Sam's truck roared toward the house. I needed a plan. I tried the back door. Surely his dad had guns in the house. Locked.

I shuffled my feet across the porch. Should I try to break the glass or run to the barn?

"Shit!" I said aloud. "Think, Ro." There might not be a gun in the barn but surely there would be a weapon. Hell, even a rake might do.

I peered out from behind the house, listening for his steps. I could hear his feet on the porch wood. Thump after thump, then the squeal of the front door gliding open. He was in the house.

I sprinted toward the barn as fast as I've ever run in my life. The door was partially ajar so I was able to slip in the crack without creating a noise. It was jet black in there. Where was the light? I ran my hands along the walls. There had to be things hanging from the walls in here. I pictured the barn of my friend from grade school. Saddle straps, hoes, metal rakes, even a few machetes had been on the walls in that barn.

I tried to orient myself, remembering the set-up of the friend's barn from my childhood.

"If the door is there," I closed my eyes and turned my body, "then the hooks were on this wall." I walked behind the door to the other wall and pressed my hand against the wood.

I heard Rusty shuffle her feet in the stall, notably curious at my presence. I felt a long object under my hand. My hand slid up. It was a broom. Not enough. I continued my exploration, heading closer and closer to Rusty's stall. Another wooden object but a shorter handle. It was a hammer. I grabbed it off the hook without a sound.

I slid back to the area just behind the door so when he opened it, I would be behind it.

Sure enough, the door started to open. I heard his feet create a whine from the wood as it squealed under his weight. The hay shuffled under Sam's feet.

Rusty let out a snort. The door opened wider and he continued in further, opening the door to the point that it echoed off the tip of my toes in a low clunk as it hit me. I had kicked off my heels from court already and had run from my car in only bare feet. I peeked out beyond the door. My eyes had adjusted to the dark by now, but his hadn't.

I saw the bulb and white string dangling from the ceiling. He was heading for the light. I eased around the corner of the door and just as he went to reach for the string, I nailed him in the back of the head with the hammer. How's that for irony, Shakespeare?

He stumbled in the dark as I darted out of the door of the barn. I hadn't hit him hard enough to knock him out. I had no idea what I was doing. All I knew was that I had to survive and not just for me but for all of the girls he would hurt after me.

He ran after me, roughly grabbing me by the hair from the back and ripping me back toward him. With his right hand, he pressed me up against the wooden fence by my neck. I could feel his fingers pressing so deeply into my skin, I thought his fingers might go right through to the muscle underneath.

I struggled to breathe, feeling my feet instinctively kicking at him in desperation. My eyes watered and I felt the pressure of the blood building in my face. It felt like he was going to pop me like a pimple.

Just then, I felt a thump against the fence. A hard thump. A thump with weight.

Sam's scream echoed for almost a mile into the night air as Rusty leaned over the fence and bit a chunk off of Sam's right shoulder. As luck would have it, that was the shoulder that was helping to hold my neck. His grip let go of me immediately after recognizing the horse's assault and I took off running. The front door was wide open now. Where would an old farmer keep a gun?

I thought back to my dad. Where did my dad keep the guns? In the place you would need it when you least expected it and when your defenses were down—the bedroom.

I ran to the bedroom and locked the door. The wood squealed as I ripped the drawers open one-by-one, jamming my fingers along the seam between the clothing and the wood. There had to be one here somewhere. I checked the nightstand drawer.

"Ro, think!" I said aloud. My eyes darted across the room for something I missed —a hiding place I hadn't thought of yet.

I looked at the bed. It was well-made with a blue, floral comforter and three decorative pillows piled on top of the pillows they used to sleep. There was a jewelry dish on the night stand to the left. A man's watch on the night stand to the right. I ran to the right side of the bed. I slipped my hand under the pillow.

"Please, God," I said as my hand lingered under the fabric. Something hard hit my thumb. I pulled it out, stunned at my own good fortune. It was a .44 pistol, an old-style Western, cowboy-looking thing at that. Long barrel. Twice as long as the barrel on my .22. That would make it more accurate. Hopefully.

I sat on the bed and turned on the light over the nightstand. The gun was heavy. I hoped that meant it was loaded. I flipped open the clip. Six shots.

"Remember," my dad's voice boomed in my ears. "Wait for them to come to you. Don't waste a shot you'll need."

I laid back on Joe's pillow and bent my left leg while I wrapped my fingers around the white handle. I steadied my right wrist on my left knee as a stand to keep my hand from shaking. I aimed for the door and just as I heard a paperclip jiggle in the lock on the door, I cocked the hammer.

CHAPTER FIFTEEN

THE CHASE

Just then, I heard them.   Sirens.
Wailing into the night, growing closer and
closer. My eyes fixated on the door handle.

"Turn," I wished in my mind.   My
right eye was already closed. I knew how tall
he was and the barrel of my weapon was
already strategically aimed. The second his
chest breached the edge of that door, it would
all be over, forever.

I wasn't sure if I was ready to do it—
to kill another person—and watch their blood
spill out all over the floor. I killed a snake once
in my basement with a field hockey stick and
even then, I screeched and apologized to it as it
wriggled and eventually gave up its life.

He let go of the door handle and I
could feel his heavy weight bounding down
the wooden steps. I held my breath. The pang
of the back screen door banged against the
house. He was the one being chased now.

I kept the gun loosely gripped in my
right hand as I started down the steps. I had
already heard the tires scrape to a stop in the
driveway.   Six police cars, maybe more.   I
stood behind the wooden door frame as I
swung open the front door. I paused before
my body darkened the doorway. I didn't want

some over-eager officer aimlessly shooting when the door opened. I hesitated at setting down my gun.

I waved an empty arm in the doorway. I heard people yelling from several yards away, telling me to step out with my hands up.

I did so obediently. With both empty hands raised, I stepped into the doorway and as my eyes processed the view, I began to sob. There were even more officers pulling in now. It was like a community carnival with all the lights and all I could feel was relief. Rusty was confused by it all, pacing in her field, trotting nervously and snorting.

"He went out the back door on foot," I yelled to them as four officers took off behind the house, guns raised.

Sam was in the woods behind the house by then. It was dark and his feet kept getting jammed up on fallen branches as he tried to run. For once, he didn't have a plan.

The officers—the real officers—were smart. One wrapped around the other end of the strip of woods while the other three flushed him out like well-trained springer spaniels.

I sat on the back of an ambulance in the driveway with a blanket over my shoulders while an EMT checked my wounds. The hand print over my neck was already starting to bruise in a combination of reds, purples and blues. I looked down at my fingers and watched them tremble uncontrollably as I came down off of the high. I could hear the muffled noises of the radio frequency emanating from the squad cars, giving me a play-by-play of the chase and my heart sank to my toes when I heard those three words.

"We lost him."

CHAPTER SIXTEEN

THE HUNT

I had officers outside of my house for three weeks, every night for the entire night. They would change shifts at 8am and 7:30pm daily, like clockwork. One squad car would line up behind the other while the first one left for home. It was a lovely feeling that I had protection just a few feet away from my front door; it was paired with an awful feeling—like I was being hunted.

I knew Sam was out there, watching me. A practiced predator, he couldn't bear to let me be the one that got away. He was probably salivating at the high he would get not only from killing me, overpowering me, watching my face as he squeezed every ounce of life out of my lungs but this murder would be unlike all the others. This one would be dripping with revenge. My life would be the reparation for all the trouble I caused him.

I had purchased another gun, a Glock 9mm, that was permanently plastered to my hip, concealed permit or not. I wore baggy shirts so no one knew I had it but me.

It was a Friday. I had finished up my shift at the office and headed home with some degree of comfort knowing I still had a few hours of sunlight before the sun dipped behind the horizon. Most nights I left the office when it was already dark.

I pulled up to my house and nodded to the officers as the garage door opened and I pulled inside. I shut off the engine, grabbed my phone and work supplies while I headed inside. I set down my things on the kitchen table and placed my keys in the small, decorative bowl by the back door.

"What a day," I complained to Luna as I rummaged in the refrigerator for a few slices of cheese. I opened the pantry and brought down a box of crackers. I ate a few standing right there over the kitchen sink.

Just as I went to take the gun off and set it down, I heard a creak from inside the house. Luna was wagging her tail, whining for me to give her a scoop for dinner.

"Shh, shh," I whispered to Luna as I tried to hear.

My fingers wrapped around my pistol and I raised it, descending down the hallway of closed doors. I typically kept them closed to keep Luna from lying on the guest room comforter; the last thing a guest wants to wake up to is a hairball in their throat. I opened the door to the guest room and nodded to myself. The comforter was perfectly smoothed as I had left it, not so much as a ripple indicating anyone had been in there.

Next room: the office. I swung the door open loudly this time. How dare he make me fearful in my own damn house. Nothing.

The door to the bedroom had been open the entire time since Luna liked to sleep in there during the day. I had planned to duck my head in quickly, anticipating nothing and that I was simply going crazy.

I heard Luna's panting on the bed. And as my eyes scanned the room, I saw Sam sitting next to her.

CHAPTER SEVENTEEN

GODDAMN SAM

I froze, gun aimed at him while my hand involuntarily began to shake. Sam Horrocks, the murderer, had gotten into my house even with a squad car parked out front. John was right. He was smarter than I anticipated.

He had my .22 pistol from my nightstand in his hand and it was aimed at Luna's head. Her sweet face stared at me affectionately. My heart leapt in my throat like that moment you almost get into a car accident but then swerve out of the way.

I instantly set my gun on the ground and let go, raising both hands. Kill me, sure, but don't shoot my dog in front of me. I'll never recover. I closed my eyes, waiting to either hear the shot or feel Sam shoot me.

I heard movement on the bed and squinted one eye open. I heard Luna's toenails tapping the hardwood floor as she got off the bed and started down the hallway. Thank God.

Sam's weapon of choice wasn't a gun —it was too impersonal and I knew that. Sam approached me while I tried to convince my feet to run. I felt his hand gently brush my hair out of the way, caressing my cheek the way he used to when we were dating. I felt his soft lips linger on the skin of my cheek, softly sliding over my delicate flesh. It sent a cold chill down the back of my neck.

As his lips neared my neck, I heard him take a long inhale of the scent of my shampoo. He had left the .22 sitting on the bed and my eyes stared past him wondering how I could reasonably get to it. Glock on the floor. Pistol on the bed. So many options but if I couldn't get to them fast enough, there was no way I could physically overpower a man.

I quickly bent half-way almost like I was leaning for the gun then whipped myself back to standing position, nailing him in the nose with the back of my head. I took off running back down the hallway, toward the back door. Holy hell did my head hurt. His eyes would be watery, blurry from the assault which might work in my favor. Even if he had the gun, he might not be able to aim it.

I darted out the door to the patio and used one of the decorative pillars that held up the patio awning to get up on the roof. I had only done this twice, to clean out a clogged gutter. It had taken me at least twenty minutes to figure out how to get up there without a ladder. Standing on the HVAC unit wasn't high enough and with the gutter along the edges of the roof, nothing was sturdy enough to get your fingers around it to pull yourself up. That is when I discovered I was light enough not to bend the metal pillar.

The roof is metal and getting up there is certainly not a particularly quiet endeavor. As he followed me out onto the patio, he could hear the metal bending and knocking above his head. I laid perfectly still on my back, invisible from ground's eye view. I heard his feet on the grass. What was he doing? The metal patio door opened and closed as he went back in the house.

This was it. I scrambled up the world's most dangerous roofing system, just waiting for one of those metal rectangles to slide out from under my foot, sending me screaming as I fell off the side of the house into what would more than likely be either an azalea or the arms of a murder. Neither sounded particularly appealing. All I had to do was get to the top of the roof and wave to the squad car.

I made it to the top peak and looked out over the street to find that the cops were not there anymore. I glanced at my watch. Shit! They changed shifts around 7:30, typically leaving after the next one showed up. It was 7:28 and one had left early—surely goddamn Sam had memorized the schedule of the officer shift change. I was on my own. I heard movement behind me and leapt into action the moment I realized Sam was clambering up the pillar to get onto the roof as well.

I had devised a plan. I needed to get Sam away from the house so I could get back to the bedroom and retrieve my gun. Sam would follow me on foot. I stood at the very peak of the roof, as far to my neighbor's house as possible. Sam and I locked eyes. Then, I jumped.

Now, my neighbors on one side were a unique specimen of white trash, never bothering to trim the bushes that were so high they were becoming intertwined with the phone lines. I figured I could grab on to something as I leapt and make some sort of elegant dismount. It didn't really happen that way in actuality.

I outstretched like a flying squirrel, trying to wrap my entire body around that bush only instead of creating some sort of resistance in return, the bush easily bent almost like I had just hopped into a pile of tall grass. I managed to stay on my feet as I wriggled off of it, sprinting down two of my neighbor's yards.

A few weeks ago, I somehow managed to lose the grip on Luna's leash and she had taken off after the neighbor's cat, down almost a half a mile chasing the darn thing. As she ran, I followed: yelling, mumbling obscenities, and watching my breath in the crisp morning air as I trotted through the neighbor's yards one-by-one in my boxers, a loose tee shirt and no bra. My one neighbor gave me a friendly nod as I jogged past, standing there staring at me with his flannel shirt, coffee mug in one hand and a cigarette in the other. I swore once I caught that dog of mine, I was going to kill her.

With that in mind, I had the advantage. I knew which yards had a dog, which ones had a fence and how to loop around, between and possibly over the shrubbery to make a loop, hopefully losing Sam in the process.

I heard Sam grunt as he jumped off the roof. He was after me now. Left to right my sneakers galloped like a thoroughbred off the thick grass, making sure not to run in a perfectly straight line just in case he did have one of my guns. I glanced back to make sure he was behind me and nearly yelped at how close he was. I thought I was faster than him.

I dipped left, turning on a dime and slipping between two arborvitaes. The Simpson's yard. I only knew that because Luna liked to pee on their mailbox at the other end of their property; their mailbox was labeled "The Simpson Family." It was roughly 300 yards back to the house now.

I blew my breath out as much as I could to inspire as much oxygen as possible with the subsequent deep breath inward. Hopefully, it would power my legs to move faster. The plan was perfectly in place in my mind now. As I rounded my street and saw my house, I ran full-tilt toward the brick. Someone watching from afar might think I was a lunatic for a moment for right before I ran straight into the side of the house, I slid.

Just like sliding into second base during my travel-team softball days, I kicked out the three-pane, Plexiglass window to the basement and squealed in pain as I came to a stop on the floor about six feet down, back-first.

I had expected the window to shatter, kind of like glass but instead it had just parted at the point of impact and as I squeezed through the hole I created, the sharp edges sliced me like a loaf of bread on the way in. Still, I was in the house and that was the important part. I heard Luna start barking upstairs. I had glanced at the street on my way in and there still was no squad car yet.

I got up and hid behind the dryer, anticipating him coming through the window after me. Instead, I heard the patio door again. Damn. I hadn't lost him and now he was between me and the guns. This was not going as I had planned. I glanced down and noticed I had soaked both sides of my scrub top in blood, bleeding from the elbows I had crossed over my face during my burst through the Plexiglass.

I wrapped my hand around the baseball bat I kept in the basement next to the dryer; it was mostly used with a few tennis balls to play with Luna in the unfinished basement when it was too rainy to go outside. I tip toed up the steps toward the basement door just outside the kitchen. I could hear my heartbeat pound in my ears.

Before I had time to prepare, he swung open the door and my bat was in motion. I hit him right in the face at first but the swing was impeded by the amount of space in the stairs. I hadn't enough room to really wind up. As he stumbled backward and I emerged through the door and into the kitchen, I let loose.

Like a beautiful, just-outside-the-plate change-up on the second pitch, I swung to the fences. His head happened to be the ball.

I threw him off enough that I had room to get to the bedroom. His nose bled like a gunshot all over the front of his shirt almost immediately. Luna had retreated, scared of the antics in the kitchen and was hiding in the dark bedroom when I got there. I reached for the Glock.

It was way too light. He had unloaded it while I was on the roof. That's why he went back in the house. I scrambled for the .22 on the bed. Also light. Shit! This was it—the moment I would see the pearly gates. My back was turned to the door like every one of his unsuspecting victims as he darkened the doorway.

I could tell by the shape of his shadow that he had his signature weapon, too. My bat.

I turned to face him and he flicked on the light and smiled at me. It was that dark smile, eyes almost black, that I bet every girl saw right before he killed her. He didn't look human anymore, not the sweet green-eyed Sam I loved. He didn't have an ounce of fear in his eyes. He thought he outsmarted me.

Wait for them to come to you. My mouth curled into a smile right back at him.

Sam had emptied the clip, but not the chamber. I had one left—the one I loaded into the barrel the day I watched the news, before any of this even started. "Don't waste a bullet you'll need."

I raised the gun and shut my right eye as Sam began to laugh at me, thinking I still had no idea that he had emptied it. My hand shook as I tried to line up my sights. I struggled to center the bump on the end of the barrel between my sights on the gun.

"Focus," I coached myself through the tremors. I envisioned the Pepsi cans with my dad, reveling in the thought of my dad beside me for comfort, guiding me and cheering me on. I thought about the girls—Marissa Bergey, Sherry Kriebel—and I thought about Jack. Justice needed to be served. I only had one chance. The second he took a step toward me, my hands miraculously stopped shaking. My sights aligned and as the tension my pointer finger created on the trigger intensified, I felt the recoil.

He stumbled backward, hitting the wall in the hallway with his back before falling to the floor. His eyes changed immediately from anger and hatred to shock, disbelief and worry. He left a red stain on my cream wall as his back dragged down the paint. After that, I watched as he tripped over Luna's water bowl struggling to get toward the back door. I jumped out the window of my bedroom long before waiting to see if he died. He would, of course, but maybe not right away.

A .22 bullet stays in the body until they bleed to death—just like my mom learned on television. By the time I jumped out the window, the squad car was there. The officer looked like he saw a ghost when I limped out into the street, waving to him. He hadn't even heard the shot.

The police retrieved Sam from my house in a swarm of officers, finding him nearly unconscious in a puddle of blood on my hardwood floors. I would never be able to fully lift the stain.

In the ambulance, they were able to stop the bleeding and in the hospital, they managed to save the bastard. All my hard work to kill him, gone.

CHAPTER EIGHTEEN

THE SENTENCING

Though I was ready to take the stand in Sam's trial, seeing him still made my hands shake as the bailiff brought him in to sit at the defense table. I could see his eyes searching the crowd for me as his feet shuffled against the cold tile floor of the courtroom. I feared he had something up his sleeve.

Our eyes met and his face contorted into that sick smile of his—mean and dark. I considered giving him the middle finger but decided to maintain some elegance of behavior.

"I'd like to call Dr. Reese Brown to the stand," the attorney announced. Dr. Brown stood from his seat next to me and casually walked to the stand. He seemed calm.

"Dr. Brown, can you express to the jury your credentials qualifying you as an 'expert witness' in the field of dentistry?" Dr. Brown fielded the question effortlessly, boasting his board-certified qualifications in addition to his clinical experience.

The attorney presented several exhibits the same way they had done when I was on the stand.

"Given the materials presented to you, including several records of service within the last year, do you find it plausible—without a reasonable doubt—that Sam Horrocks," he motioned to the defense, "committed these acts?"

"Absolutely" Dr. Brown responded immediately.

"Could you elaborate?"

"Before 2018, Sam Horrocks only had a partial denture—a removable piece of glorified plastic—to replace his missing upper right canine. Even if he had been wearing the denture when he bit those women, to create the amount of force generated to leave a mark on a human's skin, a single acrylic nesbit denture would probably move under the pressure. They're designed for cosmetics and they're designed for vertical pressure. When he made that bite, the horizontal pressure of it most likely would force the tooth forward, popping it out of his mouth." He used a prop to explain further to the jury. "What is more likely is that he was not wearing it during the assault."

"Do you find anything else unusual about his records?"

"Yes. While Sam's brother, John, was on trial for this same crime, Sam went to a dentist in Chicago immediately after learning that John's attorney had secured dental records clearing John of committing these crimes."

"So, what are you suggesting?"

"Sam knew that his attempt to frame John for these murders would not play out as he had planned so he needed to secure his own fate. He planned to falsely represent that he, too, had a permanent replacement for tooth #6 before the murders occurred. That would exclude him from being added to the list of potential suspects. He planned to present that it was impossible for his mouth to create that bite mark—assuming that no one could prove the date when the bridge was placed."

"Objection!" the defense whined.

"Speculation." Sure, Dr. Brown had just accused Sam of trying to frame his brother and the trial wasn't deep enough yet for the rest of the evidence to support that theory.

"Sustained. Please continue."

"Dr. Brown, in your expert opinion, do you believe that Sam Horrocks murdered, bit, assaulted and disposed of the five women involved in this case?"

"Yes."

I looked over at the jury that was surprisingly less diversified than the one in John's trial. They all seemed to be staring across the room at Sam. One of the women in the jury box, the only one who was African American, looked like she wanted to hit him. It was encouraging. She wore a pretty coral lipstick with her hair slicked back into a low bun, arms crossed in disbelief at the horrors of the case in front of her. I hoped she would convince the other jurors to sway in her direction because she had obviously already made up her mind about Sam.

Dr. Brown stepped down after a weak cross-examination from the defense. He patted my knee as he took his seat next to me in the pews of the courtroom.

The rest of the actual forensic evidence against Sam was scarce, honestly. He was intelligent and left very little behind for anyone to find. There were no fibers from his shirt, no prints, no bodily fluids, and other than his personal connections and friendships with the victims, it was a hard sell to the jury.

I sat alone for the last day of the trial— the day of sentencing. I hoped and prayed that Dr. Brown had conveyed his unwavering conviction that Sam was the right guy. Maureen and Joe were behind me. John and his wife didn't even bother to show up.

The judge began, spectacles blanching the skin on either side of the lowest part of his nose, just above the nostrils. "The jury finds the defendant, Sam Horrocks, guilty of five counts of first degree, pre-meditated murder, one count of attempted murder and aggravated assault. In the two counts of mutilation of a corpse, the jury finds the defendant guilty," the judge continued on, listing the independent charges as my hands relaxed for the first time in many months. I wanted to cry.

"You will be sentenced to five counts of life in prison without the possibility of parole" the judge read coldly from his paper, peering up over the brim periodically at Sam.

Mark was there for the trial, curious how it would all play out after his case with John had disintegrated. He shot me a smile.

I couldn't help but watch intently as the bailiff took Sam away. I watched every detail of it, making sure the cuffs were really locked by the way the skin of his wrists pressed against the metal as he walked. I watched his every movement, his every fiber of hair blowing in the wind of the courtroom air as he disappeared through the door, expecting him to pull some stunt again.

He sent me a series of letters from prison for a few months before I eventually moved. I couldn't risk Sam knowing where I lived or what connections he had outside of that prison—ones that might target me even with Sam behind bars. His letters were heartbreaking; some were from the angry, vengeful Sam and others seemingly from the one I loved, almost like they were two different people.

Certain letters reminded me of how much I really loved him; he described that time we went mini golfing in the summer and I almost maimed a little kid in the head with a wild shot. Or that time I tripped up the steps at a fancy restaurant and flailed around on the floor trying to get my bearings in those damn high heels. Sam hadn't even helped but rather, watched in amusement and broke out in hysterical laughter for months afterward every time he brought it up. Reading the letters made my eyes well with tears to the point that I stopped reading them altogether. When they would arrive, I would tear them in half and throw them away.

I couldn't let him hold me hostage in that purgatory of never really getting over him. It took many months for me to finally stop sleeping with my .22 under my pillow like Joe. For every aimless creak in the house not to make my blood boil with fear. For me to be open to meeting another man, letting him touch my body.

How profoundly painful it is to grieve the loss of a person still living. Knowing the one person who can take all your pain away is the same one who caused it. Feeling like you have to strain yourself just to get out of bed in the morning and do it all alone, to stand on your own two feet and learn to enjoy life all over again as if you had forgotten how.

With time, it all returned to me like riding a bike. I found a new café for Sundays with my novels, placing James Patterson back on the shelf and moving on to Scott Turow and his law-involved crime anecdotes.

The winters broke their long streaks of bitter cold, making way for spring and the fresh flowers. I soon realized that the flowers are stronger in Pennsylvania. They learn to winter. No matter how many inches of oppressive snow and ice, the hyacinths will rise again; the daffodils will surge through the broken branches and many inches of dead leaves effortlessly as they signal the rest to come back to life. And just like that, it was green again and so was I.

And when that summer turned to fall, with the yellow speckles of color along the horizon of reds as the leaves transitioned, I fell in love again.